Rachel Richards

Contents

I0670532

Prelude

Promiscuous: `...engaging in sexual intercourse indiscriminately or with many persons.' (Webster's Dictionary)

She closed her eyes and opened her mouth to let the penis slide easily between her lips. Her mouth watered around the invasive object as she let her tongue flicker its bottom. This met with approval from its owner who couldn't resist pulling it out and then ramming it in again. Again she squeezed her mouth around it, sucking it, loving it, admiring it like it was the most precious object in the world. Well, right now to her it was the greatest thing in the world. Right now this beautiful stiff penis was the most important thing in her world and the way she was now attacking it not only suggested but basically confirmed that she was losing herself in the world of lust. As her head bobbed she knew that passion was consuming her. Opening as wide as she could she happily deep-throated the hard stiff penis.

It is the little things in life that give the greatest pleasure, she thought. She then realized that this penis wasn't little. It wasn't the biggest, but it was a good size. It was the perfect size for sucking. And sucked it she did! She got into a good rhythm, her

Kelly's

Wild

Side

Rachel Richards

head bobbed to an intense beat.

It was just too much for him. Without warning, he came, jerking several times and filling the condom. Even though she knew that he was coming, it took his softness to snap her back to reality. She surveyed the situation. She was on her knees in the alley behind the bar in front of a guy who was now well satisfied. She was a little drunk and really horny.

"Shit!" She swore softly. He is useless to me now, she thought. I was too good and once men get what they want they're gone.

She was right. "Thanks babe," he said. He pulled up his pants. "That was great." And without as much as a goodbye, the stranger was gone. Satisfied and drunk he went home to sleep it off, leaving her high and…well, not dry, but very very wet.

"Jerk," she said, but he was already gone. "Selfish prick."

She went back inside to find another hard penis, but didn't look forward to going through the whole ordeal again. Fortunately, for her it wouldn't take long to find another willing participant. However, this time she was going to try to at least get something inside of her.

She felt her heart pounding faster and stronger as she became more and more aware of each breath that she took. Her lungs filled with air, tightening her chest, making her breasts feel larger than they were, before she nervously exhaled, all to the rhythm of a racing heartbeat. Even though she was drunk, her senses were on high alert and she felt the rush, felt very alive and exhilarated. To her, dancing with the unknown was the best aphrodisiac in the world and a huge mystery sat right next to her. She looked at the stocky man that she just met and smiled. Without intending to broadcast her carnal intentions, every move, look and mannerism she made screamed that she was ready to go deep into the unknown to explore passion with every part of her being.

The twenty-something guy that she had been drinking with for the past half hour had just said something, but as of this moment she was done with small talk. Leaning forward on her barstool, she softly kissed him on the cheek. He was pleasantly stunned by this sudden display of affection and when she saw that he didn't object to it, she went to stage two. She whispered in his ear, "Take me." She kissed his cheek again and her hand brushed his crotch, which instantly responded. There was no doubt that he found this as equally as exciting.

"Where to?" He asked. There was excitement in his eyes and a big grin on his face.

She looked at him and even though she wanted to be thrown on top of the bar and ravished by this bear of a man, she managed to say, "My place around the corner."

Needless to say, she wanted to get further than giving head in the back alley.

"Great," he said, "let's go." He tilted the bottom of his bottle towards the ceiling. Empty, he placed it on the bar and then made a move to leave. She didn't move.

"Wait," she said, "you do play safe, right?"

"Of course I do," he said. To prove it to her he pulled a condom out of his wallet and held it in the palm of his hand. She seemed to be transfixed by the object as she licked her lips. She couldn't wait for it to be filled with meat and slid inside of her. This was her only thought.

"Are you ready to go?" He said.

She giggled. "For hours now," she said as she flashed her bedroom eyes at him.

He gently, but firmly guided her towards the door.

Her heart was racing now. This was it! She knew that she had just boarded a ride that she couldn't stop until the end. All volition had been given away and she was at the mercy of a man twice her body weight and as strong as a bull. She had turned him on and she had no intentions of even trying to turn him off, even if she could. He had one thing on his mind and fortunately, it was the exact same thing as she. She smiled because of the way that he looked at her, and she knew that he had a whole bunch of perversions that he wanted to act out on her body.

Oh god, she thought. That was exactly what I want him to do. Go wild on me. Go wild in me. Have sex me like the slut I am.

As they walked, she let her mind wander and pictured him grabbing her to plant a big kiss on her lips. This unleashed her passion and he knew that he could do anything he wanted with her. With one move he half carried her behind a row of bushes in someone's backyard. The bushes were thick, but they covered only a portion of the view from the street. He didn't care; he forced her down onto her knees. The grass was soft and he moved behind her. He undid her jeans and slid them down exposing her beautiful ass, hidden only by her pink panties. He ripped them off and then forced her down onto all fours. With her pants around her ankles and her bare ass in the air, she waited for him. His entry was forceful and there was no question that he was admiring the view. Once in, his penis seemed to touch every pleasure point in her body at once. She voiced her approval loudly.

"Shhh!" He said as he stopped.

They both heard voices and stayed motionless as the people walked past only a few feet away on the other side of the bushes. She bit her lip as he started again. She felt him slowly sliding in and out of her. The further the couple moved away, the quicker he started pumping her. She collapsed onto the ground. Soft grass, hard penis, she thought as he grinded into her in the ground. She figured that she was going to get grass stains, but she didn't care. She squirmed and rubbed herself on the grass like a cat in heat, which of course she was.

Back to reality, her daydream was interrupted by him asking, "what are you thinking about?"

"Sex, of course," she laughed as she walked.

"Sex with who?"

"With you of course."

He smiled and increased the pace. However, as

quickly as they walked, the journey to her apartment seemed to take forever; each step was an exercise in self-control. It didn't help that every time he brushed against her, he added to her excitement. She watched him out of the corner of her eye. From the short time that she knew him, she sensed that he was a no nonsense kind of guy who won't tolerate any bull. He was squarely built, not exactly handsome, but nowhere near ugly. It looked like he was in pretty good shape, too. He was stocky, but far from fat.

They were on their way to have sex and that excited her. Oh god did it ever. Some people said that sex for her wasn't just the main thing it was the only thing. Her defense was, "hey if men can think with their dicks, why can't I think with my pussy? I love pleasure just as much as they do."

The only problem that could stop this adventure was if he refused to wear a condom or if he was into the rough stuff. Neither would she tolerate! Fortunately, since he had mentioned that he hated all that bondage crap and only played safe she wasn't worried about him. And besides, in her experience most guys who are into that crap don't bring it up until after the first time and with her, there usually wasn't a second time.

"Do you live alone?" he asked.

"Yes, don't worry, there won't be a jealous boyfriend or husband interrupting us." She laughed.

"No, I meant if you had a roommate."

"Oh god no. Hate them. I like living alone. Roommates can be such a pain in the ass."

"Don't like people much?"

"Sure I do, but only certain kinds." She smiled at him.

It didn't seem possible, but her heart beat with more force as she opened her door. It was the moment of truth. He followed her in and politely waited until she locked the door. Fortunately, he was still being a gentleman and was awaiting orders. This eased her a bit. Breathing hard, she took him by the hand and led him through the darkened living room, through the semi-lit kitchen and into the bedroom that was partially lit up by the stove light.

"Now, where is that condom?" She asked.

He produced it and she snatched it from his hand. Dropping to her knees, she helped him out of his pants. The jeans fell to the floor, the belt buckle clanging against the hardwood. She kissed the good size bulge in his underwear for luck. Then wasting no time she slid off his underwear, ripped out open the condom wrapper with her teeth, applied it, got up, took off her clothes, jumped onto the bed, opened her legs and said, "Screw me."

Inspired by her intensity, he climbed onto the bed, got between her legs and forcefully buried his penis inside of her. She let out a long moan of pleasure. He also wasn't all that quiet about enjoying the act of interlocking body parts together. He grunted with each hard stroke.

Finally getting laid, she thought. It's been too long! The waiting is the hardest part, or in my case, the wettest part. She giggled.

Her heart raced, her breathing labored, and all of her senses tuned into the events happening to her body, namely one part of her body in particular. She was very aware of each stroke as it invaded her, then retreated out of her to repeat the process. She couldn't believe how great it felt. What a rush!

I love sex! She thought. I just met this penis and it is already making me feel good, so good. In, out, in, out. In…

She thought about that nice penis that she had sucked only an hour or so ago and pretended that she was still sucking it. One of her many fantasies was to be with two guys at the same time. That way she could suck one as the other have sexed her. However as alluring as that fantasy was, she had never tried it. So far, one-night stands did it for her and she was far from being bored with them. Mostly because she knew from experience that even though everybody does basically the same thing, no one does it exactly the same way. This unknown territory was a turn on for her.

The newness of being with this new lover was driving her crazy. She wrapped her arms and legs around his body and hung on tightly, enjoying the ride. She started to pant more heavily, the intensity built, grew, and rose inside of her until she couldn't take it any longer. She dug her nails into his back and felt each hard stroke, as it seemed to rub against every pleasure spot in her pussy. Like an incoming tide, the overwhelming sensation built until it almost became too much for her to control. "Yes! Yes! Yes!" She concentrated on each stroke, loving it and wanting more. The bed creaked with every one of his thrusts, which now came hard and quick. Greedy for more pleasure her right hand slid between their sweaty bodies and she reached her clitoris, flickering just the tip with a rapid motion. The light touch teased her clitoris as his hard penis rubbed against her insides, and forced her to lose herself in the pleasure. Her head rolled to one side, her eyes clinched shut and she arched her back in an effort to capture every sensation possible.

If he hadn't felt how tight she was before, he did now. She squeezed around his meat, trying to absorb as much pleasure as possible. His penis was sliding in and out of a very wet pussy, which seemed to getting wetter and wetter with each stroke. He was inspired by her passion and increased his rhythm, and got really into it. The force of his large frame overpowered her and she moved with every thrust. As good as it felt, it still wasn't enough to make her come, and that was exactly what she wanted to do. She suggested switching positions and he obeyed. He was quickly out of her and was laying on his back, ready for more.

She eased herself onto his penis, allowing it to touch all her sensitive spots inside of her very wet pussy. High in the saddle she started riding, building with intensity with each pleasurable stroke. Again, it felt really good, but she still needed more. Leaning forward, she was able to grind her groin against his groin, rubbing her clitoris in the process. Of course, that was the point. With a penis moving around her and her clitoris being rubbed, things were getting intense. Too intense! She felt the pressure build to the point where it was getting to be too much. "Jesus have sexing Christ!" She cried.

She started panting and quickened her pace. She yelped as she came, and then groaned, "Ohhhh!!!!"

She jerked a few times as she came, and then collapsed on him, panting. However, he wasn't done. With one motion, he rolled her off him and onto her back, all the time managing to keep his penis inside of her. He started pumping immediately, turned on by her performance and craving to cum himself. Now on a mission, he rode her hard, but all she felt now was relief. A smile came to her face and it stayed there long after he came, long after he got dressed and left. She wasn't even sure if he said goodbye to her or not, nor did she care. His part was done. That penis had given her one hell of a thrill! Maybe that penis left a phone number, maybe it didn't. She didn't care. The world was filled with hard dicks who were only too willing to nail a nice piece of ass like her.

Satisfied, it was now time for sleep. In the half-light that filled her room, her heartbeat slowed until it was normal again and then it slowed even more as she happily slipped into REM sleep.

HUMP DAY

Kelly Ferguson was a svelte, 5'-3" natural redhead with short cropped hair, piercing blue eyes and a cute smile. The general consensus was that she was more sexy than beautiful, especially when she was in the mood. In the right setting, her bedroom eyes were very captivating on the object of her lust. At these times – which were frequent - the woman exhorted sexuality and it was contagious. Needless to say, finding willing partners was never a problem for her. She had the power to drive men wild and the desire to satisfy them.

At twenty-five she still adhered to what she wrote when she was eighteen. She wrote: `*God, I love to have sex men! I like big dicks, small ones, medium sized dicks, fat ones, skinny ones, circumcised, uncircumcised, you name it and if it is erect, then I like it. The only thing that I don't like is a limp dick. I have no use for someone who isn't into it/me. That is a huge turn off!*

Why? Because what really turns me on is seeing a guy hard as a rock with only one thing on his mind. It indicates that I'm driving him wild with passion. It tells me that he is mine! So give me a half decent looking guy with a strong desire to do me and I'm ready to go.'

And ready to go she was, and did frequently over

the years; however, she didn't `go' nearly as much as she would have liked. The simple fact was that she really loved having sex! Too much was never enough! Well, since she wasn't as wild as her sex drive wanted her to be she never allowed herself to experience too much sex. She had always been too shy and inhibited to be completely carefree and unapologetic about the free spirited lifestyle that she fantasized about. Also, for years she would sometimes hold back out of fear of what the people around her would think. Still, she did pretty well when she allowed herself to break free and knew how to get what she wanted when the mood struck.

Like now!

On this particular Wednesday, the desire to have sex penetrated Kelly's every thought, eventually took control and allowed only one thing to be on her mind. Because of this, focusing on work was difficult. She struggled with each task and in the end didn't do much. Well, at least she tried to get something done. The little redhead didn't know why her sex drive was in overdrive today; she only knew that for some reason she needed to get laid a.s.a.p! Maybe it was because she had been ignoring that side of things for the last couple of days – and the weekend with Doug-The-Slug wasn't very satisfying (actually the entire romance with him hadn't been satisfying and it had been a while since she had have sexed a stranger) - or maybe it was because it looked like spring had finally come to the city and springtime is the time for new love. Yuck! She hated that word! Correction: springtime is time to make love more often and with as many people as possible. That definition she could not only live with, but actually ascribed to. She knew that it was going to be a hot summer.

Staring off into space, she could see herself – well, a flawless and upgraded version of herself - lying on a bed with naked men all around her. One by one they worked hard to please her as the others waited with a number in their hands. All of them were young, handsome and in great shape. Also, unlike reality, she was sober and not the least bit shy or apologetic about her free lifestyle.

Getting deeper into her daydream she envisioned an athletic man busy grinding his large penis into her tight wet pussy as she hung onto his strong arms to brace herself. Of course, it felt wonderful and his movements were smooth and flawless. He gradually picked up speed, which caused her to lose herself to the passion. His intense eyes peered at her lustfully, making her feel like she was wor-shipped and the only one person in the world. She wrapped her long legs around him and enjoyed the sensation of having a nice piece of meat slide in and out of her. Both of her hands caressed his firm shoulders and then worked their way down his back until she was able to get a grip on his round ass, all the while he was working hard to please her. She concentrated on the movements of his penis.

In, out, in, out, she thought, god that feels so good! He's gorgeous. So perfectly built and so am I. I have long legs, large breasts and…

She arched her back to offer her large breasts to him, but was surprised by two other guys who each took a nipple into their mouths. "Sorry," one of them said, "but we just couldn't wait any longer. You are just too beautiful."

She knew that if she weren't so turned on, this day-dream would have made her laugh. It was more than a little silly. Back to the fun, the first guy increased his rhythm so intensely that it was all she could do to hang on, his athleticism really coming into play as he pounded away at breakneck speed. She was the helpless victim of his aggression. He had her so that she couldn't move even if she wanted to. The sensation was overwhelming and she came again. He growled when he came.

"That was amazing," he said after he caught his breath. He kissed her softly and then made room for the next guy to climb aboard. The next guy was quick to move in. "Wow," he said. He was completely different from the first guy. As the first was athletic, lean and strong, the next guy was just strong. He was a body builder with no body hair. She looked to the left and saw the third guy working her breasts. He was a pretty boy. She liked the variety of her worshippers and the only common ground was that they all were totally into her and that they knew what they were doing in bed. Kelly's ideal man wasn't just one man or one type of man, but it was a team of unique men that worked hard to please her.

She smiled as the body builder's large penis pointed its way towards her well-lubricated opening. It slowly pushed into her and...

"Kelly to Earth," a voice said, snapping her out of her delicious daydream.

Ugh! She thought as she re-entered reality and glared at Sara, who was standing in the doorway. "What?" she said to her co-worker. She didn't bother to hide the irritation in her voice.

"Sorry, did I interrupt a good daydream?" Her tone of voice was sarcastic.

Kelly looked at the curvy brunette then said, "A great one actually. Go away."

Sara rolled her eyes. "You know if you had sex as often as you thought about it, you wouldn't have time to work."

"Or sleep or eat," Kelly muttered.

Sara strolled into her office, stood by the window and announced, "Look how beautiful it is outside. It looks like everyone is out and about."

Kelly surrendered. She knew that her old friend wouldn't let her get back to her daydream, so she went to the window to see what she was talking about. Main Street was packed with everyone out enjoying the weather. Gone were the winter jackets, boots and the snow. It was replaced with people in clothing that didn't conceal what they looked like.

"Oh, look at him," Sara said. She pointed at a guy that Kelly couldn't pick out in the crowd. "Now there is someone who will take your mind off that novice that you've been dating."

It was just as well that she didn't see the hot looking guy because that might have pushed her over the edge, and an office filled with a dozen women wasn't the best place for that to happen. But then again, spontaneously going lesbo wasn't the worst crime in the world. She had done it a few times before and had enjoyed herself. However, the chances of that happening here were next to nil. In her opinion, this office was the most sexually repressed spot in the world. Most of the women in the office were religious and/or married with children and if that wasn't enough, dealing with single mothers and deadbeat dads all day long was enough to turn anybody off sex. However, it affected Kelly in a different way. Dealing with all the negative aspects of relationships and seeing the worst of men was maybe why Kelly only wanted the physical benefits of men. She sometimes wondered if that was why she avoided long term relationships.

Also, there was something else that scared her. She said on more than one occasion: "I never want to wind up being left with a baby and no man."

Some people labeled her as a commitment-phobe, while others only thought that she was a lost little girl who needed a man to get back on track. All she knew was that they were all wrong. Sara was about the only person who even remotely understood her.

"I'm the female stud. A confirmed bachelorette."

Whenever she stated this, most people would respond with a question like, "What about the security of having someone?"

"I'm secure in the fact that the world is full of willing dicks. Listen I'm not one of those sluts that sleeps with every cute guy that comes along. I need a reason to hook up. I like to think that I have more class than your average nymphomaniac. That is why I spend a little time getting to know them. I need to know that I'm going to be treated with respect and properly taken care of. Nice to me goes a long way."

In her day, Sara was the catalyst of most of their adventures, by supporting an almost unquenchable thirst for sex. In university she was the wilder of the two of them, daring Kelly to do things that she wouldn't normally do. It was Sara who pushed her into sleeping with other women. However, now Sara had settled down and gotten married to a sex maniac. The man could go at any time and Sara barely kept up with him, though she had lots of fun trying.

Kelly, on the other hand, was just horny, plain and simple. All she could think about was having something slide in and out of her, the harder and faster the better. She regularly daydreamed of a penis slowly penetrating her, teasing her, pleasing her.

"You're just penis crazy," Sara told her.

"And like you weren't?"

"When I was younger."

"And now you're dead?"

"Ah, no. These days I just take it home."

"How often do you guys do it?"

"Five, six times a week."

"Really? That is more than me."

"Yeah, but I have a live at home penis so it's convenient." She snickered. "I don't have to go out and find one."

"Like that is a difficult task."

"Yep. That is true."

"Men just want to have sex and the easier it is, the better for them."

"And it is the same for you."

"That is why men and I get on so well." She smiled.

"Maybe I should clone Dave for you," Sara told Kelly. "You need your own version of him."

"I'm looking," she said. "Trust me, I'm looking, but I haven't found him yet. In the meantime, I need sex. For me, the best way to clean my head of problems is sex. It takes my mind off things. I guess it gets me off in more ways than one."

"Well, good sex is the key to happiness."

"Bad sex isn't too bad either."

"How true."

"The problem with being in a relationship – no matter how wonderful the other person is – is that things – especially the sex part – fall into a routine, and routine means boredom."

"Sounds like you've had too many boring relation-ships – the sex part at least."

"Or if the sex part isn't boring, then it's just a sexual relationship that dives down into the kinky stuff, which I have no use for. It seems to be one or the other. No balance."

A co-worker who was as straight as they come interrupted their conversation. With her limp bor-ing hair, glasses and frumpy outfit, Linda looked like a librarian who had sucked one too many lemons. This sour women walked into her office and asked, "What are you looking for?"

I'm looking for the prefect screw, Kelly mused, everything from the seduction to the ultimate climax.

"The ever ready penis," Sara joked. "Keeps going and going."

Kelly glanced at the uptight Linda who took everything very seriously. So much so that it was too easy to make fun of her. Kelly saw her squirm and then

said to Sara, "You mean, keeps cumming and cumming."

Sara laughed. "Sounds like Dave."

Linda ignored them and said, "Sara. Are you coming back to the meeting? We weren't finished." She was clearly offended by the trash talk.

"Oh, sorry. I thought we were."

"Well, if you two stopped talking about men for one minute, you might be able to concentrate on what's going on in this office. We have women with real problems that need to be addressed." Linda gave her a stern look and then left.

Kelly rolled her eyes and Sara gave Linda's back a dirty look.

"You had better go before Linda spontaneously

combusts."

"And that would be a bad thing how?" Sara's tone indicated that she wouldn't mind seeing that happen.

"Oh, it would be messy. I'm not picking up all the Linda bits off the carpet and from the walls and the ceiling." Kelly laughed and Sara shook her head and smiled.

"Talk to you later," Sara said on her way out.

To take her mind off this sexless office, she tried to return to her daydream. Unfortunately, that one was gone. Instead she envisioned men's physical benefits. Big, medium and small, they were all good. In her mind, she re-sucked some that she has had in the past and got to know some she had only seen in movies.

God I'm horny! Soon, she thought. Relief will come shortly after I get home. Soon. Soon! Soon!!

Tonight, she decided everything else could and would wait. She had already blown off dinner with Doug-The-Slug and she could do the grocery shopping tomorrow, the food will always be there. Leftovers or ordering in will have to do. Her needs were too urgent. Passion had been building inside of her all day, from the moment that she woke up, all through the workday until now, where it consumed her. These sensations weren't new to her, but for some reason today they were particularly strong.

The firemen's calendar that Sara showed her at lunch didn't help…actually it did help, but in the wrong way, it turned her on even more. The effect that it had on her wasn't lost on Sara. She knew that her friend was trying to hide that she was lusting over each model. This added to an already long day for her, especially for someone who constantly daydreamed of rushing home to masturbate.

When she got home, instead of going directly to the bedroom to please herself, like she had been planning to do all day, she went into the kitchen to open a bottle of red wine, knowing full well that the stuff was an aphrodisiac that would only torture herself even more.

On the couch, she sipped her wine as she leaned back and thought of her day. She wanted to make this special feeling last a little longer, all the while letting it build. Hell, she was one step closer to exploding with each slip of red wine. She knew that something had to be done soon and was conscious not to let it go too long because these wonderful feelings would go away if they were ignored for too long.

No danger of that happening, she thought. Not with me. My sex drive is in overdrive.

At first this made her laugh and she felt very sexy before it made her feel sad. Well, guilty actually. She tried not to think of the narrow-minded prudes in the office, like Linda.

Why must they always force their monogamist life-styles onto everyone, especially me? She thought. Do I wear a sign that says, `Preach To Me'?

Except for her friend Sara, who once partied like her, she felt alone. They were the only open minded people in the office. But even the crazy hard partying

bi-sexual Sara had settled down now and…Kelly felt alone, very alone in her perversions.

For company, she decided not to have another glass of red wine – that would only push her over the edge – but a beer instead. She recited a chant from university. "Liquor before beer never fear. Beer and then liquor, never sicker."

The first beer was quickly followed by a second and then a third, so that by the time that she changed into her jeans and tank top she was already pleasantly buzzed. The jeans and the tank top weren't the sexiest clothing that she could wear, but it would do. Anyhow, she usually shied away from being the center of attention and preferred to slip quietly into a room rather than make an entrance. Shyness was her nemesis. However, drunkenness was now her inspiration and tonight she was well armed. She was soaked in more ways than one, drunk and wet.

Looking in the mirror to check out her attire, she knew that she was good looking enough that most straight men would have sex her even if she were wearing a potato sack. Apparently, it was her eyes that captured men. She had been told that she has bedroom eyes. That worked for her. Right now, the plan was to use them.

She finished the third beer and wondered why she always had to drink before she did this. I'm too messed up to have sex sober, she mused. I wish that I could be free. She momentarily felt sadness as she remembered what Sara had said about having a live-at-home penis. Yes, deep down she wished that she could find someone like that. It would be nice to come home to something like that and…she stopped herself.

"Screw it!" She said. "Hmmm…have sex me. I'm drunk."

She giggled.

She placed the empty beer bottle beside its two friends on the counter, grabbed her purse and keys and staggered out. A few blocks from her apartment was a good pub and she knew that it would start to fill up soon. It was one of those Pub chains that advertised that each location was slightly different and one was right for you. They all had different first names, Pub being the last. This one, she referred to as the Pussy Pub because it was the most happening singles bar in the neighborhood. Well, maybe it wasn't, but it was filled with guys, her kind of singles bar; no competition.

Quietly she snuck in, got a seat at the end of the bar and checked out the scenery. Two of the best looking guys were at the other end of the bar. One was Matt the bartender and Kelly admired the back view of his perfectly styled blonde hair. Her eyes traveled down his well-toned body covered only by a pink t-shirt and a tight pair of jeans. She must have been staring at his butt for too long because the guy that he was talking to noticed her and indicated to Matt her presence. He was a customer who she had never seen before. Not nearly as pretty as Matt, but still better groomed than most straight men. She looked away as Matt broke off the conversation and got back to work.

"Sorry about that Kelly. The usual?" Matt asked.

I wish that he wasn't gay, she thought as she made eye contact with the pretty boy. "Please," she said. His friend was probably gay too. He was taller, broader, had a square jaw and she was thinking that he looked kind of straight. She thought that maybe she and him could hook up, but then saw his eyes travel up and down Matt's body. He checked Matt out as much as she had just done.

He's gay. Won't get anywhere with him, she thought. Well, at least we both have good taste.

Next...

As she looked around the room she noted every guy, but she wasn't interested in one enough to be satisfied. One guy knew that he was downright good looking, but guys like that were not her type. She knew that she could never be comfortable with their egos. Several others would do, heck, they all probably would do the job. However, she figured that she had starved herself for this long, so she might as well get someone who would be better than okay. She wanted someone who knew what they were doing and who wanted to please her. Someone who was confident, experienced and had a good body that was strong and muscular with no fat. Ugh! God did she hate a potbelly! She didn't care how big a guy's penis was. If his belly cast a shadow over it then forget it.

Hmmm dicks, she thought. Images of some of the beautiful dicks that she had sucked flashed through her mind. Midway through her drink, she started to feel the full effects of too much alcohol and not enough physical attention. She was a little drunk and very horny, the perfect – actually, the only – combination for her to get picked up and have sexed by a total stranger. This couldn't be done sober.

She knew that she had spotted 'him' when her heart rate quickened and she was conscious of her breathing. The candidate was playing pool with a buddy. He was about 5'-9", short dark hair, pleasant looking, thin but with some muscles. When they locked eyes she knew that she would be naked with him soon. He broke off eye contact first as she lustfully peered at his physique. He said something to his buddy, which was probably to tell him that he was going for drinks and headed her way. She smiled when he walked straight towards her. Under the pretense of ordering another round he stood beside her, like it was the only space available at the bar.

"How are you?" He asked her after he had ordered.

"Very good," Kelly said brightly, "and you?" She was very conscious of each breath she took and her heart drummed out a strong steady rhythm.

"Doing fine. Name's Rob. What's yours?"

"Kelly." She squinted and stared directly into his eyes, transmitting her desires to him. He was quick to pick up her message.

After trading small talk with him for awhile, she had him pegged as a fairly decent guy, intelligent enough, definitely not an abusive type. He's just a nice guy who wants to get laid, she thought. Say, I can help him with that. I'm just a nice girl who only wants to get laid.

"I've never seen you here before," he said. "New to the neighborhood?"

"I come here all the time."

"Really?"

"Yes, but I never stay here for very long."

He raised an eyebrow. "Why is that?" There was a little tension in his voice.

She laughed. "Oh don't worry, I'm not a working girl, if that was you're thinking."

"Oh, I wasn't thinking that," he said, now tension free. He was a bad liar.

Not wanting to tell him that she just came here long enough to find someone to get naked with, she said, "Oh I just live a few blocks from here. I usually meet friends here for a drink or two."

He glanced around. "So are you meeting someone tonight?"

"Yes, I did. She just left and I was just finishing my beer."

He bit his lip and nodded. "Can I convince you to stay a little longer? What would it take?"

She took a deep breath and tried to slow down her racing heartbeat. "Usually a beer, but...maybe I don't want to stay," she said playfully. She looked directly into his eyes and she was enjoying this now, her senses working overtime. So much so that she let her left hand stroke his leg. She giggled and continued to let her hand brush against his leg.

"So...if you don't want to stay, do you want to go somewhere else? And if you do, you want some company?" The line wasn't delivered very smoothly. It was clear that he wasn't a player. This only confirmed to her that he was just a guy who wanted to get laid. He was her type, easy to control and not a threat.

"It depends."

"Oh what?"

She leaned over and whispered in his ear, "If you treat me with respect. Which, to start, means that you're willing to wear a condom."

Instantly, he knew that he was in and said obediently, "Of course I am. Anything you want. Anything."

She smiled. "Good boy. Then my place it is." She tilted her glass up to finish off her beer. "Let's go and find out how good of a lover you are. Say goodbye to your friend. I'll meet you outside."

"Okay." He left.

She saw that the bartender was talking to his boyfriend again and it appeared to be quite the intense talk. Not wanting to interrupt, but wanting to be polite she said, "Goodnight Matt. See you soon."

"Goodnight Kelly," he said. His friend raised his glass to wish her a good night.

The reason that she wanted to meet him outside was that she didn't want to see Rob receive a high five from his buddy and all that macho boy crap. And besides, she wanted a few moments alone in order to steady herself. She momentarily asked herself what she doing, but convinced herself that all will be fine. Rob was a nice guy. She breathed in the cool night air and looked skyward. This relaxed her.

That was a quick pick up, she thought. However, her body was saying that it wasn't quick enough.

The sound of the door opening brought her back to earth. She saw him flying out of the door, eager for beaver, and this excited her. She could barely contain herself as they walked down the street together. So much for her trying to collect herself. If he had thrown her into the bushes and tried to do her right then and there, she wouldn't have put up a fight. Secretly, she wished that he would.

Her place was a few blocks in.

"Mine's the top apartment," she said.

"You live alone?"

"Yes."

Inside, after she had locked the door, she told him to have a seat, but he grabbed her instead. He kissed her and she kissed him back. A wave of pleasure overwhelmed her from every place where he put his hands. The sensation moved as his hands went from her waist to her rear. The little redhead closed her eyes, wrapped her arms around his neck and enjoyed being groped.

"God, you have a nice ass!" He said.

"Thank you."

Before she knew it, her feet were off the floor and he effortlessly carried her towards the back of the apartment where he assumed the bedroom was. After a wrong turn into the bathroom he found the bed and gently laid her on it. He kissed her neck while undoing her blouse.

She was surprised how easily he got her bra off and didn't stumble like most guys. He cupped her left tit while he sucked her right nipple.

"Your nipples are huge!" He said. There was excitement in his voice.

"You like them?"

"I love them!"

As he sucked a nipple, his right hand traveled down her body until it got to her jeans. She moaned and opened her legs. This was one of many signs that indicated that she wanted to get her brains have sexed out. He slowly, but firmly rubbed her through her jeans while teased her nipple with his tongue. She tried to absorb as much pleasure as she could.

She didn't know – or even cared – how much time

passed before he shifted to stage two. With both hands he undid her jeans and slid them off her. Her panties were next, leaving her totally naked as he stood over the bed studying her body as he undressed. As she stared lustfully at him, she gave him a full view of how she masturbated. Her right hand was flickering her clitoris while her left massaged her nipples. Her eyes told him that this felt good. Very good!

She looked up and was happy when to see that he was in the process of putting on a condom. The size was average, but satisfactory to Kelly. It pointed straight towards her and this pleased her. He was giving her the `you're number one' sign.

He saw her nod with approval at the application of the condom. "As you commanded," he said.

"Good boy!" She was breathing hard now.

He shook his head. "God, you're the horniest thing that I've ever met. How long has it been since you've last had sex? A couple of years?"

She looked at him, smiled and said, "Less talking, more fucking!"

To back her words, she repositioned herself so that she could take his penis into her mouth. Hungrily, she attacked it. He groaned as the softness of her lips and tongue covered the condom-covered penis with saliva. She let herself go and got into a rhythm. It was the same quick solid rhythm as her heartbeat.

"Stop or I'll come," he said.

She laughed and pulled away. "You better not," she commanded. She started to play with herself again.

He removed her hand from her crotch and gently placed it over her head. Not so gently, he forced his penis into her. She gasped as felt his aggression. He was soon pumping hard.

"Yes, that's good," she said.

"Girls like you need to be fucked hard!" He said.

She didn't protest – as if she could disprove that fact – and decided to just enjoy the best part of male aggression. She moaned with every hard stroke. This was her favorite position, to be flat on her back with a hard penis inside of her with a gentle, but dominate man at the controls. It was very good, but not enough. She knew that she wanted to get off; she would have to lend a hand or two. While her left hand played with her taunt nipples the index finger on her other hand flicked her clitoris. At first it matched the rhythm of Rob's penis pulsating in and out of her then it sped up as she slipped off into fantasyland. Now it was some handsome guy with a great body on top of her. She couldn't make up her mind if it was Brad Pitt or a number of other hunks. Finally, she made a decision and it was all of them. One by one they rode her. As they took over she muttered. "I'm a slut, I'm a slut…"

Hearing this Rob rode her harder. He watched her lose herself in the passion and grew harder, the hardest that he had been in a long time. She soon had a nice little orgasm. She had a couple more and it wasn't long before the instrument of her pleasure exploded inside of her.

"How the mighty…" maybe not so mighty, she thought, "…oak has fallen."

He rolled off and laid there satisfied. She didn't care if he passed out or left. He would either be gone now or in the morning.

She lay there feeling satisfied and ready to pass out.

Shit, the alarm, she thought and that realization snapped her back to reality. She sat up and started to set the alarm.

"What time do you get up?"

"Five." She lied, hoping that it would make him go home.

"Shit that's too early for me," he said. He got up and started to dress. "Sorry, but..."

"Hey, don't worry about it. We met, we screwed and so be it. Don't promise to call me or anything if you don't want to."

"Really, but..."

"Like you said, a girl like you..."

"Ah, sorry I didn't mean it like that."

"Well, it's true. I'm a slut. I love getting it on with total strangers."

He was a little shocked. "You do this often?"

She was going to say, "No, not really. I've been seeing this guy for the last few months and it isn't really working," but decided to say instead, "A few times a week."

"Anytime with the same guy?"

"Of course. I have a few dicks that I drain on a regular basis."

"Can I have your number?"

"So you can come over have sex my brains out and then leave?"

He was blown away by her frankness. "Ah…"

"Actually, I would like that." She smiled got up kissed him and saw him to the door. Before he left they exchanged numbers. As she was closing the door, she said, "Rob."

He stopped. "Yeah?"

"Thanks for a good time."

He looked pleased with himself. This was a night to brag about for a long time. "Anytime, babe. Anytime."

She locked the door and felt like she was already asleep as she staggered towards her bed.

UNIVERSITY DAYS

The alarm came too soon and was far too loud for her sensitive head. Before she was even able to open her eyes to turn off the invasive noise, she knew that she was in rough shape, sexually satisfied – for now - but hung over, very hung over. "F'ing hell," she groaned then silently cursed herself for drinking far too much last night. She turned off the alarm and laid back down. She couldn't put the overwhelming feeling of surrendering to total pleasure out of her mind. She loved sex and to her too much was never enough. Someone once asked her what she liked about it, to which she replied, "What don't I love about it?"

There is some sort of gene inside of almost every female's brain – or at least there was inside of Kelly – that craved to please to a man and was only satisfied upon seeing that she has done so. It seems that as long as this gene is satisfied, they usually don't need to orgasm. Well, not as often at least.

Kelly seemed to have an oversized gene of this type. She found it particularly gratifying when she sexually satisfied a man, from getting them aroused to draining them of all of their sperm. The fact that it was usually a different man every time didn't change things for her even though she secretly wished that she could find the prefect penis…err, make that the prefect man. Still, getting a man off, any man, made her feel contented.

"I like making people happy," she once said to a friend. "Guys are very happy when they cum. They love me for it."

"But that kind of love is fleeting," the friend answered. "It's not meant to last."

"Hey, I'll take it. It's still love. At least I'm spreading love around."

"Oh, is that what you call it? More like spreading your legs around."

"But isn't that what guys want? A quick easy have sex?"

"Yes, but what do you, want? Don't sacrifice your happiness for strangers."

"Sex," she said matter-of-fact. "And plenty of it."

And speaking of sex…she had lots of fun last night. Like an athlete who goes over each play in her head, she replayed last night's have sex in hers. It didn't take her long before her hands found her vagina. The fingers of her left hand spread her lips apart as the other slipped into her moisture. First it was one finger, then two and then finally three as her right hand mimicked his penis as it thrusted in and out of her. The thumb of her left hand teased her clitoris as she squirmed and moaned. After her orgasm she felt back to sleep.

The phone rang at 9:20 and she knew that it was Sara calling from work. Her friend knew her habits well and acted as a second alarm. Kelly both loved and hated her for doing this. With much discomfort, she got her ass out of bed and reluctantly began the day.

At breakfast she thought of Rob and wrote this below his number in her equivalent to a little black book. She called it her "Dicksinary":

Penis – average size

Technique: dominant and a rough rider, probably

from lack of experience and/or training

Looks: pleasant

Summary: will do again if convenient

Considering how much her head hurt, she was in a good mood – she always was the next morning after a good lay. Still, something bothered her and it was more than feeling guilty about dumping Doug yesterday and then having a one-night stand with Rob. It was when he said: `Girls like you.' She had no problem being a horny little nympho, but she didn't like it to be so obvious. Then again, allowing herself to be picked up in a bar by a total stranger certainly didn't do anything to hide her sluttiness.

The simple fact was that she enjoyed doing what she did last night. Hell, since she broke it off with Doug-the-limp-dick yesterday, she wasn't cheating on anyone or afraid to commit or anything like that, it was just sex. And sex is all that she wanted. Rob was a decent guy who was all too glad to be given permission to stick his thing into her and run away with no strings attached. They both got what they wanted and nobody got hurt. She was comfortable in the fact that when a guy came along that was worthy of committing to she would gladly give it a go. Hell, she had done that in the past more than a few times. One relationship even lasted three of her twenty-five years. That was Brian and was two years ago. She tried not to think about the fact that she had gotten bored with him and was glad that it had ended. In fact, she may have even sub-consciously destroyed their relationship, but she wanted to believe that she was capable of commitment. However, she did like to play with new friends.

I like playing with their dinkies, she thought.

Reading, `Looking For Mr. Goodbar' by Judith Rossner a few years ago made her all too aware of the dangers of picking up total strangers and more than once she went home alone when she was unsure. Because of her training and experience, she was good at reading people and if she couldn't figure them out then she didn't trust them. No trust, no have sex.

What she wasn't good at was not feeling guilty about it. She wished that she could block out all those voices that shouted their ultra conservative opinions at her. Her mother, sister and some of her friends were amongst them. Maybe that was why she had to drink before she picked up. It helped block out those voices until the next day. Now sober, the voices formed a choir. She was forced to listen to their tired old songs. To counter it, she kept busy by getting ready and rushing off to work.

She was late for work, but nobody really noticed. This was part of Kelly's lifestyle and everyone knew that she could make up the lost time.

Sara gave her a few minutes, and then came into her office. "You look rough girl,' Sara said. "Did you even get his name this time?"

Kelly blushed. "Yes, and he even left his telephone

number."

"Was it worth it?"

For the first time this morning, Kelly smiled.

Sara looked envious. "Good."

"Thanks for the second alarm."

"You're welcome."

When Sara left, Kelly heard the choir again. They sang a song that told her that she shouldn't have drunk so much on a weeknight, or on any night for that matter. But I can't get the courage if I don't, she thought.

She hated herself for that and for being such a tramp. The choir sang, `Amen."

At lunch, she told Sara the details and like she had all during university, she listened. Only now Sara had settled down, so there weren't any recent stories to tell, so unlike university, she gradually veered the conversation back to shop talk. Kelly only half listened to Sara as she told her all the problems she was having with one of her cases. Normally she would have paid more attention, but today Kelly was a hurting unit. She was sluggish and had a hard time eating with all the noise in the cafeteria. Every bang was felt.

Kelly realized that working in the office was affecting her more than she realized. She decided that to have a baby with a man would leave her too vulnerable. Still, she wanted to keep in practice at this baby-making thing. God! She really loved to practice. She couldn't help but pay more attention to the men walking by than to her best friend. She realized that she was out of control.

After dinner that night, instead of watching television, she laid down on the couch to think, or – as she put it – to sort out her life. Of course, she didn't really like her body, but she knew that most men considered her to be sexy. This might have had to do with her sultry attitude and natural redhead mystique.

"Redheads exhume sex," someone once told her. "It is common knowledge that all redheads love sex and you're no exception."

She was petite, thin, but not skinny. Svelte would be a better description. Like a lot of women she wished that her breasts were bigger, but that would make her flashy and she wasn't about that. That would attract the wrong type of man. No, she was about quietly meeting a nice, average guy and giving him something to brag about to his buddies. Like Rob the other night. He was good for her ego, making her feel not only wanted, but in control, too. Also, it was nice to generally please a man. There must be something to that. I've made a number of men very happy over the years. What is wrong with that?

To her the big question was: but have I made myself happy?

She closed her eyes, took a deep breath and knew that she had to look back to properly examine her present. She remembered:

She lost her virginity the day after her eighteenth birthday. She had waited because of what her mother and her church were saying. Both demanded that she wait until marriage and she listened to them until she realized that they were nothing more than pleasure haters. One day she heard a song on the radio that had a line about rather be laughing with the sinners than crying with the saints. She made up her mind right then and there that she was giving it away to the next boyfriend she got. She would at least try this sex thing. This way she could make up her own mind instead of believing someone else's biased – and probably jaded - opinion.

She met Mark at a party and things heated up quickly between them. On the way home he took her parking and he easily had her in the back seat.

His hands were everywhere as they kissed. So far she liked having her breasts touched and her ass grabbed.

Hmmm...she thought, I like being touched.

He lifted her blouse, undid the bra and took a nipple in his mouth. She moaned. A hand parted her legs and worked its way up her inner thigh. She parted her legs. When he touched her crotch she gasped. She couldn't believe how good that felt. He rubbed her the right way for a few minutes until she said, "Take me."

"Gladly."

The pair of them undressed as best as they could in the cramped backside. Naked, she laid down on the seat with her legs spread. He slowly pointed his penis towards her and she braced herself. She was prepared for the first time to hurt. That is what she had been told to expect, but it didn't. As Mark slid it in (he was clumsy of course, but he wasn't too overbearing size-wise), she braced herself for the pain. There was a little, but it soon turned to pleasure. Pure pleasure! Mark got an earful of how much she loved it and quickly was so overwhelmed by the sensation and her expressive moaning that he came.

"Sorry," he said.

"That is okay, just don't move."

"Ah…why?"

"It feels good having you in me."

After a few minutes, Kelly started to worry about the condom leaking and/or falling off. She was just about to say something when he got hard again.

"Can we do it again?" He asked.

She said, "Yes, but we better check the condom first."

"Better yet, I'll use another one."

He had it off and another one on in record time. His enthusiasm turned her on. She opened her legs and waited for him. He almost lost another load when he saw the passion in her eyes. He said, "You really like it, don't you?"

"God, yes!"

He smiled. "My little baby likes to have sex."

Kelly looked at the ceiling and felt his presence inside of her. She closed her eyes and came to the conclusion that it felt very good. "Yes, I love it," she said.

Mark and Kelly basically had sex for the next year or so. They were doing it sometimes as much as four or five times a week, trying different positions, while drunk, sober, high, straight, indoors, outdoors, anywhere, anytime that they could manage to be alone together. She was addicted to his hard dick and he always had one.

Things changed when she went off to university. It wasn't her choice to leave home, but because of the distance her parents insisted that she live on campus. She was depressed about leaving Mark until she got settled in school. Walking around campus she spotted men of every size, shape, color and attitude. She knew that hidden in their pants was a hard penis that she was dying to get inside of her. And it wasn't long before that happened. The first Friday night she went to the pub with a few female classmates that she had met. It wasn't long before her attention strayed from the girl talk to the guys around the bar. Before she knew it, she was in her room being ridden by a guy that she had just met and had gotten her drunk. He was bigger than Mark, but not as good. It could have been that they were both too drunk to enjoy it. Or it might have been that Kelly and Mark got to know each other's desires very well and knew exactly how to please each other. Still, the excitement of being nailed by a total stranger was exhilarating.

He wasn't there in the morning and she felt terrible

in more ways than one. She was so hung-over and felt very guilty. She had cheated on Mark within a week of getting there. Well, they both knew it was going to happen, it was just that she couldn't believe that it happened so soon.

I'm not even here a week, she thought, and already I act like I don't even miss him.

She stopped her thought process and stared at the ceiling. Slowly, a realization came to mind. She and Mark had lots of fun, but it was done. Circumstances forced them apart. He was now a two-hour drive away and she didn't have a car. He had already said that he would do the drive, but that it wasn't practical to visit more than once a month or so. They both agreed – without really saying it - that it was over, no hard feelings.

She was now a fulltime resident of an adult playground. Welcome to a world without parents where young men and women, drugs and alcohol are thrown together in an unrestricted mayhem. In this world, she was free to do whatever she wanted. She could sleep with whoever she wanted to. She smiled as she threw the guilt aside. She certainly enjoyed conquering that guy last night. It was like the hunt. Spot the prey, stake it, and then take it. She couldn't wait to go hunting again.

First sleep to feel better, she thought. Then awake to start a new life.

By four she had managed to get up, grab breakfast/lunch and lay down again. One of her classmates she had recently met came to her door. She let her in and down she went again.

"You okay?" Sara asked.

"Fine, just a little catnap."

"So what happened last night with that guy?"

Kelly didn't know to tell her or not, so she didn't say anything.

"Come on tell me. I'll tell you," Sara said. "We did it in the backseat of his car and, my god, he had the biggest dick! I swear that it reached halfway to the roof."

Kelly giggled. "Donkey boy. The best kind of ride."

Sara exalted. "I just stared at it. It was huge."

"Did it hurt?"

"Yes."

"Sorry to hear that."

"I didn't really mind. Fortunately, it didn't last long. It was worth it. So what happened with you?"

Kelly told her what she could remember, which wasn't much. She had drunk far too much and didn't oppose his entrance into the fun zone.

"You didn't like it?"

"Oh no, I liked it. Sex is fun. I just wished that I didn't drink so much."

"Want to go out again tonight?"

"Sure, but I'm not drinking nearly as much."

"How about the have sexing?"

"That's why I don't want to drink that much. I want to remember the fun part."

"You slut!"

She laughed and looked devilishly at her new friend. She didn't know why she was opening up to Sara as much as she was, but she felt very comfortable with her. "Yep. I like to have sex." Kelly did a cat stretch, smiled and added, "The part that I like the most is seeing how much the guy wants me and just how far he will go to have me. And of course, how good it feels." She closed her eyes. "I don't understand why some women don't like it. It feels awesome."

"It certainly does."

Kelly and Sara on average picked up – or in most cases – allowed themselves to get picked up, laid and then forgotten about roughly three times a week. Usually twice every weekend and maybe once during the week. They became good friends in their mutual perversions. None of their other friends shared their open views and soon they learned to keep certain things to themselves.

After a while there were a few regulars who visited Kelly during the week, but

no one special enough to give up the others for. That was until George. They went together for most of the winter. At first, it was like Mark all over again, going at it like rabbits, but by March things started to slow down and Kelly got bored. It wasn't long before she started with the one-night stands again and by summer break, they were history. For the summer she went back home and she and Mark picked up where they had left off. In September she was back at school and free again. She couldn't have advertised that fact more if she wore a sign that said, `Very available' or `Permanently wet'.

During the first pub night, she joked to Sara, `I should put up an advertisement that reads: `Horny slut available for parties, one night stands and open to anything hot and wild.'

Rachel Richards

"How much would you charge?" Sara asked.

"I'm free to a good bone."

Sara laughed. "I like that one. Mind if I use it?"

"Go ahead. It's your motto as much as mine."

Sara looked at Kelly and smiled. "Okay soul sister, what is the wildest thing that you've done?" She asked.

"You mean besides picking up a total stranger and draining his dick?"

"Yes."

"I'm not sure."

"Ever been with two guys at the same time?"

The expression on Kelly's face was that of shock. "You can do that?"

"Yes."

"And the guys don't mind?"

"You're so naïve at times. So I guess that means you haven't?"

"No, I haven't. You?"

"No. Nor have I ever had a threesome or four-some."

"Me neither."

They talked about their experiences with men as they bought their own rounds. By eleven Kelly was pretty loose and the place was getting crowded.

"Kelly? Can I ask you something?"

"Sure."

"Ever been with a woman?" Kelly stared at her. It wasn't that Sara was bad looking – actually she was quite attractive – it was that Kelly didn't think of her in that way. Well, actually she did a little, but she valued her friendship too much to risk it on cheap sex. Kelly had always admired her long willowy brown hair and hourglass figure, wished that she had large breasts like Sara's, but it stopped there.

"Don't worry, I'm not coming onto you. We're just talking."

"Okay. Well to answer your question, no, I have haven't been."

"Have you ever considered it?"

Kelly reflected on this. "With an endless supply of dicks around I've never given it much thought. Why, do you ask? Have you?"

"Yes."

Kelly was mildly shocked. "And?"

"It was good. Very different."

"I take it that this happened over the summer?"

"Yep."

Sara told her what happened and it really shocked Kelly. It surprised her even more when Sara said: "I dare you to pick up a woman tonight."

"What?"

"Instead of the usual guys, let's pick up a few women."

"Ah…who?" She sheepishly looked around.

"You know that girl Sharon across the hall from me?"

"Yeah. She just walked in a few minutes ago."

"She's queer."

"Oh, how do you know that?"

"I've seen her bring home a woman and then listened outside her door as they screwed."

Now, Kelly was shocked. "Sara!"

"I've been watching and I've noticed that there is a little lesbo crowd – they're very quiet about it, but they usually hang out at the far end of the bar. Want to change locations and see if we get hit on?"

"Are you serious?"

"Yes. Come on try it, just once. If you don't like it then a solid diet of dick it is for you from now on."

"Oh, I don't know. I'm not bi."

"How do you know? Have you ever tried it?"

Kelly glared at her as if to say, "You know that I haven't. Heck, I haven't even thought about it be-fore.

"Tell you what. If you try it and if you really hate it then you can borrow my ghetto blaster for a week.

"Really? This sounds interesting."

"Promise."

Playfully, she upped the ante. "A month."

"Okay. Now you must be honest and give it a true chance."

Kelly sighed. "Okay." Even the walk to the back of the bar Kelly found to be nerve-racking. They got a table next to one filled with Sharon and her friends. "I need a drink," Kelly said.

Sara kept looking at Sharon and it didn't go unnoticed by Kelly. "Oh that's it. You just want an excuse to screw Sharon. You have the hots for her."

"Yep."

"And you dragged me into a voyage to the Isle of Lesbos."

"Yep. Enjoy the scenery."

Sara went to the bar and waited, making sure that her large breasts were in good position to be noticed by the girls at the dyke table. She made sure that she made eye contact with Sharon. As expected, Sharon joined her and as Kelly watched this all take place, she knew that she wasn't getting a drink anytime soon. Frustrated, she went herself. She was just far enough away to give Sara some space. She returned to the table and felt alone.

This sucks, she thought.

She was in the process of trying to finish her beer when she heard a voice. "Looks like your friend won't be back for awhile," the voice said. "Want some company?" The voice belonged to a busty blonde, one of the women that had been sitting with Sharon. She was pretty but a little rough, not butchie, but not a typical woman. She wasn't as soft and pretty like Kelly was, but was better looking than most men. The big problem for Kelly was that she didn't possess the equipment that Kelly lusted after. However, she decided that anything was better than sitting alone. "Sure, why not?" She watched her sit down.

"I'm Lisa."

"Kelly." She finished her beer and put the empty bottle on the table.

"Can I buy you another drink? You look pretty thirsty tonight." She glared lustfully at Kelly.

She nodded as she stared off into space. "If you buy them, I'll drink them."

The dyke smiled. "Back in a minute."

Lisa came back with four beers. "Here is one," she said. "And I'll take one. If you can drink two before I finish one then you can have the third."

This was no problem for Kelly who was trying to get drunk anyway and was good for Lisa, who was trying to get Kelly drunk. Sometime after listening to a lot of bitching about everything from lousy Profs to the lack of proper ventilation in the women's washroom – and a few more rounds – later, Lisa decided that she should escort Kelly back to her room.

"I'm fucking smashed," Kelly announced to anyone that was listening. She was staggering so much that Lisa had to put her arm around her to steady her.

"Which room is your?"

"121"

Lisa put her down on the bed then proceeded to take off Kelly's shoes. Kelly looked at her strangely. "What, are you queer?"

"Yes, I am."

Kelly seemed surprised by that. "Really?"

"Yes. You knew that." She said somewhat defensively.

"Oh yeah. I guess then that you want to fuck me, right?"

"Yes, I do. Is that okay?"

"Sure. You have to drive because I have no idea what to do with another chick. Dicks I know. They get hard and it's easy to get them to blow up real good." She laughed.

"Don't worry, I know exactly what to do." She lifted Kelly's blouse. "Get undressed." She did and laid on the bed with her legs spread. "This is all I have to do for the boys. Oh and to tell them to put on a condom."

"Looks very nice."

A serious look came on her face. "Lisa."

"Yes?" She was almost undressed.

"Put on a condom." Kelly giggled.

Lisa chuckled. "You're loaded."

"Yep."

Lisa stripped and climbed onto the bed.

"Holy shit you have big breasts!"

"Thanks."

Lisa laid on top of Kelly and kissed her. It took a few moments, but Kelly kissed her back and was surprised by how soft and smooth her lips felt. She put her arms around Lisa and enjoyed the attention. Slowly the experienced woman worked her way down to Kelly's breasts. Kelly's large nipples were a pleasant surprise and were thoroughly admired, which translated into plenty of sucking and licking. Kelly did not mind this, nor did she mind that while this was happening Lisa massaged her inner thighs. By the time that Lisa had moved on – or down – Kelly was soaking wet. She moaned her approval with each lick. At the hands – or tongue – of someone who knew what they were doing, Kelly felt the intensity build. She panted and squirmed as the woman's arms wrapped around her thighs to hold her in place. Feeling restricted Kelly had no choice but to accept the assault of the woman's tongue on her clitoris. At this point she no longer cared – or remembered – that it wasn't a man between her legs. Relief came in the form of an intense orgasm.

"Oh shit, that was amazing," she said after she caught her breath.

"Thank you."

She was shocked that it was a woman's voice she heard. Oh right, she remembered. I've gone lesbo tonight.

She passed out and in the morning, Lisa was gone. Actually, she thought that Lisa had left soon after her conquest, but wasn't sure. Nor did she hear the lesbian add another notch to her lipstick case. Kelly had been someone's conquest again.

"So do I keep my ghetto blaster?" Sara asked the next day.

"Yes." Kelly smiled.

"Right on."

"Yeah, well…"

"So?"

"Girls are fun, very good in fact. I'm a little disappointed that I couldn't do much for her. Actually, I don't think that I did anything for her. I was pretty drunk so I can't remember if I did or not. Come to think of it, I don't think that I did anything for her."

"Well, you did spread for her, right?"

"Yes."

"That's enough for some people."

For the third year, Kelly and Sara got an apartment in town. It was on the top floor of a house that had been renovated to be a self-contained unit of two bedrooms, a living room, kitchen and a fairly large bathroom. Their private entrance was a long wooden staircase at the side of the house. Downstairs lived a quiet couple in their thirties, old folks by their standards.

Once settled Sara stated the obvious, "We must break in the apartment."

"Sounds like a plan."

A few hours later, they walked in with a couple of guys they had just met. Kelly had her eyes on David, the muscular football player. Beers were opened and before they were drunk, Kelly was making out with David on the couch and Sara was doing the same with Bill on the floor. David's right hand held Kelly's waist firmly and he moved his lips from her lips to her neck. Arms flung back, and eyes shut, she absorbed as much pleasure as possible, soaking in his every kiss and caress. His strong hand firmly moved from her waist to cup her breasts. She let out a soft moan, and arched her back to push her tit into his hand. He stopped kissing his neck to concentrate on undoing her blouse. She squinted her bedroom eyes at him.

"No bra?" He said.

"I like the way silk feels against my nipples. It really turns me on." She didn't try to sound like Marilyn Monroe, but she was breathing so hard that she couldn't help but to sound breathless.

He believed her. He saw how erect her nipples were. In relation to her small breasts they were huge. He sucked one of them as her hands explored his broad shoulders and arms. That was nice, but she waited for his hands to start rubbing her down there.

Taking the initiative, she said, "sit back big boy. Oh, and take off your shirt."

He obeyed and she knelt before him. He unzipped and took out his penis. He was a little smaller than normal, which probably explained his devotion to weight lifting, but she liked it anyhow. She was very drunk and horny and he was very erect. All the ingredients required to get turn her on.

In the middle of the coffee table was a cookie jar filled with condoms. Kelly retrieved one from there and put it on David. Then she took his pants off and sat on his dick in record time. He was easy to get in and his lack of size didn't take away from any of the pleasure she would normally feel. Actually, because she was basically in the sitting position, she was able to rub her clitoris against his pelvis. He covered her ass with his large hands and helped her move. Every time that she rode her hands over his muscles and his six-pack she got hotter and hotter. This caused her to ride harder and moan louder.

But theirs weren't the only sounds of pleasure in the room. On the floor, just on the other side of the coffee table, Sara was also getting banged. Bill had her in the missionary position and was going to town.

"How are you doing girl?" Kelly asked Sara.

She didn't hear or chose not to answer. Her eyes were clinched and she was somewhere else.

Kelly watched Bill's athletic body grinding away. She enjoyed the view and shifted a little on David to get a better view of Sara's pussy swallowing and spitting out Bill's dick again and again. David also shifted to watch the action below.

"Okay, let's get back to it," she told David after a few minutes.

She quickened the pace; paused a bit to have an orgasm and then resumed the pace. She went up and down twice, then rocked it a few times from side to side, and then repeated. She was in a groove and before she could come again, he did.

Judging by the primal yell, Bill finished up soon after.

After everyone caught their breath, Bill started to dress and David reached for his clothes.

"Beer?" Sara asked.

"We shouldn't. We have football practice in the morning."

"Oh, you guys don't want to do it again?" Sara looked disappointed. "I thought that we could have a couple of beers, then switch up the partners or something."

Kelly was shocked by this, but also aroused. She looked at Bill and smiled. The guys stopped dressing.

"You girls are a lot of fun," Bill said.

"Pretty f'ing wild," David added.

By the way he had said that Kelly realized that she

had just screwed a biff. He isn't too bright, she thought. Bill seemed like the smart one of the pair.

Sara came back with four beers and Bill took two and brought one to Kelly who was cuddled up with a pillow on the couch. He opened it and handed it to her.

"Thank you!" She said.

He sat on the couch between her and an almost naked David, who feeling a little uncomfortable by his presence relocated to the chair. Sara sat on his lap. Bill faced Kelly and said, "Cheers."

"Cheers."

"Are you cold? Do you want a blanket?"

"No, I'm okay. Thanks anyway."

"No problem." His eyes were studying the areas of her body that the oversized pillow wasn't covering

"Something tells me you want to fuck me."

"Oh yeah."

"Whenever you're ready."

"No. Whenever you're ready."

She smiled. "You're such a gentleman."

She put the pillow behind her, laid down on the

couch and spread her legs. Her eyes were screaming, "Take me."

"Oh, I see that you're a natural redhead."

"Do you like?"

"I love it." His words were muffled because he had pressed his lips against her inner thighs and kissed. He slowly worked his way towards her red hair. The sight of red public hair excited him and he gladly went down on her. Kelly, of course, was all too willing to be admired in this fashion. Like most men his age he didn't really know what he was doing, but he was enthusiastic about the job at hand and that in and of itself was a turn on. After awhile she told him, "Screw me," of course, he obeyed.

Kelly and Bill had sex on a regular basis for the next two years. Kelly really liked him because he was a very nice guy who treated her with respect, even when he was banging her in the women's washroom of the local Harvey's or in the backseat of a car. Wherever they did it, he was a gentleman about it. It was like Mark all over again, but without the commitment. No commitment, no jealousy, just mutually rewarding hot sex. Both of them slept with other people, but they never let it interfere with their time together. Kelly was sorry that they both went their separate ways after school. She moved to Toronto and he moved to Vancouver.

She missed him – or the idea of having a steady partner – shortly after she moved to Toronto and tried to find someone like him. She dated and went through a series of relationships, all of which were short lived. Some guys were good in bed, but were total jerks, while other guys were sweet, but limp dicks. Ugh! The guys, who had both going on, eventually discarded her for reasons that she couldn't figure out. She figured that she just wasn't good enough for them. Soon she gave up on relationships, though she still dated in hopes of finding someone, but more times than not, she didn't.

Fortunately, she was still open to the idea of finding a steady guy and was still young. In the meantime, she was going to have fun and for most of the time she did. However, after a few years of having fun, decided that she needed a change. Not too much, just a tweak or two. Nor had she had any regrets about all the cheap sex she had. In fact, the process of remembering turned her on!

"I'm a promiscuous women," she said, allowing her words to echo throughout the apartment. Words that no one else heard.

As liberating as that was, it still stung. With thirty approaching, she wanted to settle down a bit. She decided that it was time to grow up a little. The first step was to cut down the drinking, but the thought of cutting back on the sex didn't sit well with her. In fact, a quick check informed her of how wet she was.

"Okay, new plan," she said to her reflection in the television. "Starting tonight I'm going to screw guys until I find one that can keep up with me. I will encourage them to see me again. Well, the good ones at least. " She smiled.

With a purpose, she got off the couch to get dressed, but before she got to the bedroom, the phone rang. She was about to pick up when she spotted the number. She knew who it was and what they wanted. However, having a quickie with a married guy was not what she wanted right now. She let the phone ring as she walked back to the bedroom.

Just before she walked out the door, the phone rang again. This time, she picked it up.

DRYSVILLE

Nervously, she walked into the Pussy Pub. She had walked into this place dozens of time without too many problems, but tonight there was one major difference. She was stone cold sober. She felt herself sweat and each move towards the place felt like she had the eyes of the world upon her. Earlier on the phone with her old high school friend, Sonya, she said, "Half the fun is taking the time to dress up, knowing that you look really hot. Then going out to turn heads." Then adding playfully, "then slowly getting undressed is pretty wild too."

"And you don't really care who does it to you?"

"As long as he has a hard dick then he is putty in my hands. Then I will force him to be a gentle-man."

"Ugh! When are you going to give up the one night stands?"

"Tonight. Now I'm on a quest for a live at home dick."

"Really?"

"Yep."

Sonya was elated by the news. She started thinking out loud whom she could set her up with.

Kelly cut her off. "I have to get ready to go on my quest."

"Hi Kelly the usual?" Matt, the gorgeous, but very gay and hence unattainable bartender said. Not a good choice for the live-at-home dick. Great for cleaning and shopping but...

"Ah, no. Just a..." she didn't know what to order. "...Ginger ale."

Matt was stunned. "Really? What you're the DD tonight or something?"

"Sort of, yeah."

He raised an eyebrow. "Okay."

She looked around, but didn't really like what she saw. Instead of seeing a room full of walking penises she only saw a bunch of guys. Still, some were pleasant looking. She felt tense and normally by now she would have forgotten about her appearance. She knew that she look fine, but for some reason was incredibility self-conscience. She just didn't feel sexy. Yes, she wanted to have sex, but she needed a reason to. Maybe, Mr. Perfect will be here tonight, she thought. And since I'm sober I won't blow it.

Matt returned with a glass of ginger ale. "It's on the house."

"Ah...thanks, but I'm not really the DD."

"No problem. You're just not in the mood tonight. It's good to slow down sometimes." He smiled at her.

"Yes. Thank you."

She decided that L.A.H.D. (live-at-home-dick) didn't make a good acronym so she came up with L.I.T. or Live-In-Tool. She told this to Matt who quipped, "Yes, he could hang nicely in the workroom with all the other tools." This made Kelly howl. Once, she had stopped laughing she said wryly, "A that tool would be used often, very often."

Matt smiled then seriously said, "Forgive me for saying, but I got the impression that you have a somewhat high sex drive."

"Oh come on, don't be polite, say it. I'm a damn nympho."

He smiled. "Oh good." As soon as he said that the look on his face suggested that he wished that he could take those words back.

"What?" She said.

"Nothing."

"Matt," she said sternly. "Cough it up."

"Again forgive me saying, but I thought that you were a pro."

"Really?"

He squinted his eyes. "Yes sorry."

"Well, I'm not one of those. I'm just a slut."

"Sorry I didn't mean to offend you, it…"

She smiled. "Don't worry you haven't."

"Really?"

"Yes, no problem."

Another customer came in and Matt left to attend to him, leaving Kelly alone on the barstool where she felt exposed and somewhat embarrassed by what Matt had said. Maybe he shouldn't have said what he had said, but she couldn't fault him. She just hated the impression that she had created. For the first time she wanted to change. It took her a few minutes before she could muster up the courage to check out the room. There were maybe a dozen people in the room. A couple was playing pool and the others seem to be grouped at tables. She was the only person sitting alone and she hated that. In a crowded room, it wouldn't have been so obvious.

Sometimes it takes patience, she told herself as she

concentrated on emptying her glass. Between sips she thought of penises and tried to get herself inspired. It didn't work. Fortunately, the place was starting to fill up. She was nearing the bottom of the glass when a guy came over and offered to buy her a `real' drink. He was average height and build with blonde hair and a hard face. Still, she thought that he wasn't near ugly. He was a possibility.

"No thanks," she said automatically.

"Are you sure? It will loosen you up."

"I'm loose." She knew that she was very tense, almost to the point of having an anxiety attack. Matt's words still stung and the choir was warming up.

"No you're not. If you are loose then let me buy you a drink."

He's too condescending and pushy, she thought. "No thank you." She turned away. He knew that he had turned her off.

"Sorry, I didn't mean to piss you off." Even his tone was condescending.

"Well I'm not drinking tonight," she said without looking at him.

He looked at her and his face fell. He left without

saying a word. She knew that she had not been herself with him. She had been cold and distant and had not given the guy any encouragement. Still, she wasn't sorry that he went away. She couldn't picture being with a jerk like him.

Next, she thought.

She looked around the room and every time that she made eye contact with a guy, she looked away. Why she did this, she wasn't sure. Maybe it was because she felt unsure of herself. She felt a little uneasy. She sighed.

Fortunately the place was now busy enough that she no longer made her feel like she stood out. She took a deep breath and tried to unwind.

"That guy is a loser," a male voice said. It came from her right. She looked at him sitting several barstools away and smiled. She figured that he must have come in within the last few minutes. He came over and continued, "I've been watching him for awhile now and he seems that he can bully his way into a woman's heart. He's had no success that I've seen. That approach just doesn't work unless the woman is completely desperate."

"You got that right."

"So, can I buy you a drink?"

"Oh, sorry. I don't drink." His face fell, clearly discouraged, but the smile came back to his face when she added, "But that doesn't mean that I don't want to talk to you." She made a mental note to change her response in future to, "Yes, but something non-alcoholic please."

The conversation was going well for a while, but as he drank more he didn't

seem to be as nice or interesting as she first thought. She concluded that normally she would be as – if not more –drunk as than he was and might not have picked up on these facts. Stone cold sober, it was a problem, it was too clear that he just wasn't that good of a guy. This became especially clear when he said, "You know I have a big penis and I know what to do with it."

Even though they were talking about sex, she did-n't like the comment. "Listen," she said. "Shut-up. Do what you're told and you might get laid, okay?"

"Yes."

She was in control now, but she knew that it wouldn't last. All the blood seemed to have trans-ferred from one head to another and the head that was talking was a real dick. It only had one thing on his mind. Which normally would be fine, but he was a crude dick.

This guy just isn't doing it for me, she thought. Or am I just being too picky?

"I'm so good you'll be bragging about me to all of your friends."

That did it. Now, she knew what she wanted and it wasn't him. She politely told the guy that she had to go and as disappointed as he was, he didn't protest much. When he asked for her phone number, she shook her head and said that her boyfriend wouldn't like it.

"What is your boyfriends name?"

"Richard Hardy."

She wasn't really lying because she saw every straight male who could get a nice hard on as her boyfriend. In the context that she saw them, they were all basically the same, but talk about variety.

Matt understood the joke and suppressed a snicker.

"Goodnight Matt," she said. "Thanks for the pops."

"Goodnight. Remember pops are always free for you. See you later."

Once home, she sat on her couch and thought about things. She had failed in her mission to have sober sex. It wasn't because she wasn't horny enough, it was that she just couldn't let her guard down and was turned off by all the creepy barflies. She hoped that these jerks weren't the normal type of guy that she usually picked up. To her disgust she knew that they probably were. It was a sobering conclusion. Now, she knew what she really wanted. That would be a sex maniac with class.

Still, she had that overwhelming desire to have something stuffed inside of

her. Maybe it had to do with the fact that she was at her most fertile time and

nature wanted her to reproduce. Her body craved being penetrated and seeded by a man, but her mind saw the wisdom of avoiding getting pregnant. It was a conflict that was overwhelming her and in order to appease both parties, she decided to continue for the perfect penis, her L.I.T. She thought: I just have to keep trying. I shouldn't need to get loaded to have sex.

The more she thought about it the more she thought that she shouldn't do it cold turkey. I could have a few drinks to loosen up, she thought. However, I know that once I start I can't stop myself. I have a glutinous personality. I love have lots of booze and sex. Too much is not enough. Hedonism is my favorite word. The more sex you have, the more you want it.

To take her mind off things, she retrieved a video from the cupboard. She turned on the television, slid the video in and took off her pants. She just managed to turn the volume down before the video kicked in. Instantly, a chorus of moans from several men and woman filled her living room. She didn't like porn that much, but she loved this video. It was one of the few that weren't too phony and just made to make money. This movie was made in the seventies and actually had a plot to it and the actors seemed to forget about the camera and just had fun.

She leaned back, rewound the tape to her favorite scene. On the screen a sultry redhead was riding a dick with much enthusiasm. Beside them was another couple getting it on. The redhead leaned forward and her and the other woman started making out. There was passion in their kisses that excited Kelly. "Nice," she said.

As she watched the changing of partners and the different combinations, positions and passions, it didn't take long for Kelly to bring herself close to orgasm. Her moans matched the actresses and wished that it was her in the video enjoying herself. All that passion, she thought, all those beautiful bodies intertwined and touching each other. Enjoying…feeling…

cumming…

One hand massaged the opening of her pussy while the other hand rubbed her clitoris, not too hard just enough to tease it. This felt good and she opened her legs wider, which caused her to slide down to where she was almost horizontal, barely able to see the television over her body. She raised her head in time to see a penis showering someone's belly with cum. This inspired her to ram a few fingers right inside of her, even though it felt good, she wished that it were bigger. Looking around she spotted something that would be better. Unfortunately, the phallic looking saltshaker was on the other side of the room.

If I get up to get it I might as well just get my vibrator, she thought. Oh, I might as well get it.

She got up and as she walked to the bedroom she took off the rest of her clothes. With her vibrator in hand she ran back into the living room naked. She enjoyed the sensation of running naked and jumped over the back of the couch to land on it. With the only L.I.T. she had right now, she laid down and eagerly spread her legs. Soon there was a hum as she guided the tool in and out of her. Like the real thing she swallowed the fake penis with enthusiasm. The setting was on medium and that was good for now. Any faster and she would cum too quickly. As she have sexed herself she tried to picture every penis that had visited her. God, there were a lot.

I've been penis crazy for a long time now, she thought. So many beautiful hard instruments of pleasure since Mark. Which one was the best?

She turned up the tool to high and remembered sucking one guy in the back of a bus. It was night and...the imagery and the sensation overwhelmed her pleasure circuits and she came.

Panting from the brief, but intense workout, she turned off the VCR and the television and stared at the ceiling. That was good, she thought. And very much needed. Maybe I should just screw myself more often.

She was zoning out when the phone rang. Without thinking she picked it up and said, "Hello?"

"Hi Kelly," Doug said. "You sound out of breath."

She wished that she hadn't picked up. "I...er...had just ran for the phone."

"I called earlier, but you weren't in."

"I went for a walk," she said, not lying. She did go for a walk, straight to a bar.

"Where to?"

"Out." She sounded irritated. That told him to change topics.

"Listen. Can we talk?"

"We are."

"I mean face to face. Can I buy you dinner tomorrow?

He had gotten her at a vulnerable moment where she was feeling lonely and she couldn't believe that she was even entertaining the thought. A rough gameplan ran through her head. Have dinner and if it didn't work out – which it won't – then stay out, get hammered and nailed by my future L.I.T.

"Kelly?"

"Ah, yes."

"Are you going to give me an answer."

"I was thinking…"

"Well, let me sweeten the pot," he said. "I have something to say and I think that you're going to like it. So, say yes. I mean it is only dinner. You have to eat."

Reluctantly she agreed. However, being pursued did cheer her up a little.

She went straight from work to meet Doug at the restaurant and like he said, he was waiting outside. As usual he was a perfect gentleman and it reminded her about why she started to see him in the first place. Also, he looked pretty damn good. He was tall, in good shape and had an almost baby face. Kelly was definitely attracted to him and wanted to ride him all day long. Unfortunately, that is where things fell down, so to speak. It was also the only topic that she wanted to talk about and he was avoiding. Topics like religion and politics were rehashed and Kelly didn't seem to mind talking about nothing until desert. However, she wondered what he had to say and why he didn't get right to it.

"How is work going?" he asked.

"Fine."

"Anything different?"

" Every case is different."

"So you'll think that you will stay there?"

"Until I retire."

"How is the mat leave there?"

"Don't know, don't care."

His mouth opened and could only say, "Really?"

"Yes, really. I don't want kids. You know that."

"But don't women who love sex only like it because it will lead to making babies?"

At first, she hated him for his narrow-minded statement then thought, good. The door is open. "I don't know about other women, but for me, I love sex because it feels so damn good and it is exciting."

"You sound like a guy."

"Why should it be different for a woman. I like sex. I never want to stop having it."

"Kelly?" He said with a serious tone.

Uh-oh, she thought. Now what? "Yes?"

"I think that there is something you should know."

"And that is…"

He leaned forward and whispered: "I think that you're a nymphomaniac? I'm not sure, but…"

"No shit Sherlock."

"Then you admit it."

"Yes, I do."

He looked sad and nodded his head. Then bravely he said, "They have treatment for that. Knowing that you have a problem is more than half the solution. Together we can overcome it."

She laughed. "Why the hell would I want to change?" She looked directly into his eyes. "I am who I am and I love it. Take it or leave it." She snickered and licked her lips. "Take me or leave me."

"I don't want to share you with other guys."

"Then you have work to do," she said seductively.

Out of the corner of her eye she saw Matt's friend walk in with some other people. He was with another guy and two women. At first she thought that it was a gay and a lesbian couple having dinner together, but then she realized that it might be two straight couples. Maybe he isn't gay after all, she thought. Hmmm…interesting.

Doug spoke again. "I'm willing to learn, but I must confess I feel that I can't measure up."

She eyed his crotch. "Oh the size of `him' is just fine. No problem with the size of your equipment."

He blushed. "I mean, I don't think that he, I mean I can...well, I'm not a porn star, I can't go for hours and hours like I think that you want. You never seem to be satisfied."

From across the room, Matt's friend spotted her and for a moment their eyes locked. He sort of smiled then his attention shifted to the blonde that was part of their party. Kelly watched her for a few moments and concluded that she must be high maintenance. To Kelly, the blonde certainly had an air about her that Kelly hated instantly.

Her absence wasn't lost on Doug. He felt like he was losing her. "I'm willing to try," he said. "After all, I do like it. I guess that..."

As he rambled on, she checked out the other woman. She was also blonde and flashy. Why do guys go for the skinny blondes with too much make-up who act like their gods gift to men? She knew the type and their `You can only have me if you spend lots of money on me' attitude.

Her inner feline instincts hissed at the blondes and their dumb slaves. Only her eyes were acting like they were paying attention. Her mind was somewhere else as Doug was still rambling on. After a few minutes, her eye caught another familiar face. Oh my god, she thought. What is his name? Aw...

I'm sure that I've had him.

When he saw her, he smiled. She smiled back. Rob, that's it, she said.

"Listen Doug," she said, interrupting him. "I'll give it one more go. Let's go to your place afterwards."

He seemed to be happy with that. However, he looked to where she was looking and caught Rob raising his glass to her. Busted, she was free to echo the sentiment. "An old boyfriend?" He asked.

"Yes."

"How long did that one last?"

One night, she thought, but said instead, "A few dates."

"Kelly," he began like he always did when he had a serious question to ask. "Since we're being totally frank and honest, can I ask how many guys you have been with?"

"Oh we are. Well then, let me start by saying that guy over there was a one night stand that I had a couple of days ago."

He was angry. "You mean that you've cheated on me?"

"No, I didn't cheat. We weren't a couple then and to be frank, we still aren't. At no time have I ever said that I was exclusively yours. You only assumed that I was. You invited me out tonight under the pretense that you had something to say to me. Something that you said that you know that I would like and so far you haven't mentioned a word about it. We've talked about everything but."

"Yes that is true." He looked hurt. "What would it take for you to commit? Are you even capable of commitment?" He glared at her.

"Yes, I am." She looked up to notice that both Matt's friend and Rob had been watching the intense whispering going on between her and Doug. She concluded correctly that both of them could size up that things weren't good between them. Heck, anyone paying attention should be able to decipher that they weren't having fun.

Acting like a desperate man who was down to his last round he was bargaining his terms of surrender. "Well? What would it take?"

"You really like me don't you?" Kelly said. Then after a pause added, "Or is it that you can't stand the fact that a woman doesn't fall at your feet and yearn to give you whatever you want? I'm sure that there have been many girls who have done that."

He was offended by her bluntness and Kelly knew

it. "Sorry if that was a little strong, but tell me the truth. You're used to girls worshipping you. Now, I have to admit, you do have a lot of wonderful qualities that make any woman sit up and take notice of you. You certainly are a good looking guy."

"Thank you."

"I mean that. So tell me...why do you keep pursuing me? What is it? I'm the one that got away?"

He looked at her. "You're an exciting woman. Smart, good looking and...unattainable."

"So that's it, isn't it? You want what you can't have."

"No, that's not it."

"Are you sure?"

"Well...maybe."

"Well, you've had me plenty of times."

"I've had your body. I want your heart. Tell me Kelly, who has your heart; that guy over there? How about him? Or her?" She glared at him as he continued to attack her, "No one. Not one of them. Sure they all can have your body, but not one has your heart. Emotionally you're the ice queen."

To her, he had just crossed the line. In a stern

whisper she said, "Listen, I don't need this. Think what you want but you can't bully me into committing to you. Thank you for dinner. Goodnight." She got up, gently pushed her chair and very quietly stormed out of the restaurant. She did it with such grace that only a few people even noticed her leave.

Out in the street, she looked both ways and wondered how the hell to get home from here, or better yet, how to get to the Pussy Pub from here to get hammered and nailed. I'm going to get loaded and if some jerk wants to help me to do it then he can fuck my brains out, she thought.

Retracing her steps, she started towards the subway, keeping an eye out for a taxi, but the streets were empty. Feeling like a weight had lifted off her shoulders, she tried to forget about Doug-The-Slug. It was unfortunate that it had to end like that, but at least it had ended. She decided no more phone calls, dates or even acknowledgement of his existence. This pleased her. Still, she felt bad for him. Not a lot, but a little.

He'll get over it, she thought. He's a very good looking guy and he'll be a lot better off when he meets someone else. Someone who would tell him that he is the best lover in the world and give him plenty of babies.

This moment of wisdom was quickly replaced by a panic attack. She wondered if she would be better off. Did she want to be single for the rest of her life? Maybe that is why she hung onto him for so long. He wasn't her ideal, but at least he was someone. She knew that she didn't want to spend her life alone. The tears started and she had to stop walking. She was trying to dry them when a car pulled up. She wasn't surprised that it was Doug. He seemed to be happy to see her crying. "So you do have a heart after all," he said.

"You're a fucking bastard," she said, "Do you know that?" She kept walking.

Keeping pace with her, he managed to steer and lean out the passenger window. "I'm sorry. I overdid it. I said too much. I was out of line."

"No shit!"

"Let me take you home."

"No. I don't think that I want anything to do with you."

"I don't blame you. I deserve that. Listen, as an apology, let me drive you home. If you want we don't have to talk."

She glared at him over her shoulder like she was being tempted by the devil.

"Listen, sit in the backseat and I'll act like a cab driver. Please, let me take you home. And besides, you don't want to ride the subway after you been crying."

She stopped. "Fine."

He stopped the car, got out and was about to open the back door when she said, "I'll sit in the front."

He opened the door for her and she got in. He drove in silence until she spoke. "Why does the world make me feel guilty about having sex?"

"I didn't mean it that way. Listen. What I wanted to say to you is that I guess that I'm a little frustrated because I don't seem to do it for you. I really like you and I want to please you, but I know that I don't. So tell me what to do and I'll do it."

The tears started again and she looked away. It was true. Here's this great guy for the taking and I don't want him because he is boring in bed. Maybe I can...no, I've tried that already. His drive just doesn't come close to mine.

"It's just..." She broke off that thought. She gave up and only looked out the window. At least the tears had stopped.

It wasn't until he turned onto her street that she spoke again. "Doug you're a great guy and I really regret that it isn't working out. Go find another girl, you will give her commitment and babies and make her very happy. I'm really sorry that I can't be happy with you. "

"Why not?"

She shook her head. "It is just not working out and I'm sorry."

"Me too." He stopped in front of her house and turned off the engine. "I don't want it to end like this."

"If you want we can have a farewell session."

"I'm not sure about that."

"Well, truth be told, if you don't do it with me, then I'll just go out and find someone who will. So why don't you come up, we'll have a few drinks and have some fun."

"Is that what you want?"

"Yes, I would like you to jump me."

"Are you sure?"

"YES!" She got out and added, "Come on."

An hour later, she was on her back and he was riding her like Doug does, slow and steady. Even though the feeling of his dick sliding in and out of her felt nice, she wished that she had more to drink because she was becoming dry. He's just boring, she thought, like a machine. Let's see, whom would I rather be with. Hmmm…how about most of the cast from Ocean's Twelve…oh yeah…or…

The more that she fantasized about other men the wetter she got and the more that she rocked underneath him. However, what really got her was when she thought about the orgy she would throw if she could. She thought of all of those beautiful bodies intertwined, touching, sucking and screwing each other. She pictured herself down on all fours sucking on a penis while some guy was sliding out of her as somebody was eating her. She had no idea who it was doing what to her, but the feeling was overwhelming. So intense, so…good! That did it and she came as Doug kept his pace. Seeing her come caused him to speed up a little. He soon came too.

He rolled off her and she felt tired.

"You seemed to enjoy that," he said. "Anything that I can do?"

"No. I'm good."

"Just checking."

She cuddled against him and he gladly held her. He started to talk and she said that they would talk tomorrow.

She fell asleep in his arms. Tomorrow she would tell him that it was over – even though he was welcome to come over for the occasional fuck - and not be wishy-washy about it. Tonight, the ice queen needed to be held.

LOOK AT ME

Somewhere between the bar and her place, he turned into a bit of a jerk, but then again Kelly was usually hammered and horny as hell at this point, so with her viewpoint normally clouded she wouldn't have noticed that they all could have been jerks. Now with her senses sharp and working overtime, she couldn't help but to notice a few things about her latest pickup. First of all, it was rapidly becoming obvious that he really fancied himself. Granted, with his movie star good looks and well-toned body he was probably the best-looking guy that she has ever met, and definitely was the hottest thing that she had ever picked up. He was gorgeous and he knew it. Maybe, he was a little too confident.

She had gone against one of her own rules by even talking to him, but he had the nicest blue eyes, the warmest smile and did all the right things and she had melted. In the bar, she had been more nervous than normal, but he soon made her feel comfortable enough to leave with him. Or maybe it was because she saw him as more of a long term than a quickie and was shooting for the stars. However, on the way home she gave up any thoughts of seeing this guy again, never mind a L.I.T. After having some fun with him that is.

He's probably the playboy type, she thought. He likes conquest. Getting in and out. Fine. That suits me. This female stud is in the mood to conquer a Greek god and then move on.

Another thing in his favor was that he wasn't Doug, who by the way didn't take it too well when she lowered the boom on him this morning, but at least he accepted it. Well, for now he did and so far hadn't called. In the meantime, she wanted to be with anyone but him. Anyone! Because of that 'incident' with Doug she decided to temporarily postpone her quest for a L.I.T.

She decided to get back to the walking work of art. During his pickup, he had told her that he has done a few commercials, one of which she had actually seen. It was at that point that she realized that was where she had seen him before. She must have been a little too impressed because that gave him the upper hand. From that point on he gradually started acting like he was more successful and better looking than Brad Pitt. By the time that they got to her place he was almost unbearable. He was more vain than Warren Beatty.

"So I said to…" He said.

She tuned out his name-dropping and concentrated on opening the door. Not that it required a lot of attention; it was just that it was more interesting than listening to him. Also, her nerves were in need a distraction. While handling the keys she noticed that her palms were sweaty.

I hope that he's a better in bed than he is a talker, she thought.

"Drink?" She said, not sure, nor caring if she was interrupting him. "Have a seat." She pointed to the couch then disappeared into the kitchen.

"Martini."

She laughed, hoping that he was kidding. "Sorry, no can do. How about a beer?" She needed one or twelve. Sobriety sucks, she thought. Then decided to give sobriety the night off.

"Ah sure." He sounded not only disappointed, but also partly condescending.

Pretension is this guy's middle name, she thought. I hope that he isn't this bad all the time. No one can be. Blame the alcohol.

She opened a beer and downed it in record time, not caring that she was making him wait. In an effort to relax, she took a deep breath, held it, and then released it slowly. She repeated then was ready to go back in.

With only the dim table lamp on – preplanned before she went out – she came back into the living room with two beers. He was sitting in the middle of the couch leaning back with his arms stretched out.

"As I was saying," he began as his audience placed the beers on the coffee table. She sat beside him wanting him to just shut-up. He was beginning to turn her off, which was very difficult to do considering that she had been wet since that morning. She let him ramble on as she gazed at his beauty. He wasn't easy to tune out, but at least he was very easy on the eyes so she was distracted. Admiring his strong shoulders, six pack and large package got her back in the mood.

"Kelly?"

She snapped out of her lustful trance. "Ah, yeah?"

"Are you listening?"

Shit! She thought. I've been caught.

Without hesitation she leaned over and started to grope him.

"Listen stud," she said. "You've already impressed me enough to get inside my panties, so you don't have to work it any longer, as long as you're willing to wear a condom, you're in."

"I'm up for it." He said then laughed at his own joke.

"Are you?" Her ideal was a nice guy with a good size and hard penis who knew how to use it and was free of society's trappings. As she felt his dick through his pants she knew that he was meeting at least one of her ideals. He was hung! Normally, she had to go on a mission to search out the guy's penis – sometimes taking too long to find it – but with him she couldn't help but to find him. He was everywhere! She palmed him up and down his shaft. Big!

"God, he's huge," she muttered. She rested her head on his chest, closed her eyes and intensified her strokes. He lifted her blouse, undid her bra and was working on her jeans when she pulled away. She stood up leaving her pants on the floor.

She ordered, "Jeans off now."

He obeyed and she kneed down in front of him. Staring directly in her face was one hell of a bulge. It had stretched his underwear to the breaking point.

"I'm a little bit on the large size," he said. There was pride in his voice.

"No kidding." Slowly she slipped off his underwear and took in the view. She smiled. It was the biggest penis that she had ever seen. Well, except in a porno. This guy could be in one, she thought, and be the <u>big</u> star. Actually, maybe he's done a few.

"Aren't I the biggest that you've ever seen? All the ladies say that I am…"

Yes, but, "Ugh!"

"…feel free to measure me."

You probably measure yourself all the time ego boy, she thought but said instead, "Less talking more fucking!"

"But I only…"

"Shhh!"

She led him by the hand to the bedroom. She momentarily thought of leading him by the dick, but she knew that he wouldn't get the humor in it and it would only blowup his overblown ego more. But at least - in her opinion - he did have something to brag about.

God, he is just big and beautiful, she thought as she walked beside him. Now here is a guy that has something to egotistical about.

At the bed, he grabbed her to kiss her and she

leaned back in what she called the surrender position. Her head was tilted, back arched, one hand around his neck and the other on his bicep. She was his prisoner and he had now been given control. He grabbed her ass and she was momentarily airborne. Before she knew it, she was flat on her back in the center of the bed and he was ripping off her panties. Once off, his hands were everywhere and his touch was warm and exciting. She closed her eyes, smiled and moaned.

Then it stopped. She waited then felt a presence beside her on the bed. She opened her eyes to see his penis waving in her face.

"It needs to be sucked," he said.

"Well, I need to be eaten," she said.

He looked sad before a realization hit him. "A sixty -nine?"

This was obvious to her, but she found it funny that genesis boy was all proud of himself for coming up with it. "Get on your back," she ordered.

He obeyed and his hard penis pointed towards the ceiling. It is so big that I could use it as a stepladder to change the light bulb, she thought wryly.

She swung a leg over him and backed into his face.

When his tongue made contact with her lips it caused her to moan. "Yes."

Unfortunately, that was the best part. His technique was monotonous and conservative. It was like he didn't care about pleasing her. His tongue stayed in one spot and he licked like a sleepy animal drinks water, slow and steady. She had always thought that such a good-looking guy would have more experience in eating pussy. She expected better.

Starring her right in the face was this penis. Big! Thick! She started her lick from the base of the shaft and slowly went up, and up and up until she got to the head. It took as long as an elevator ride up the CN Tower. She giggled at the comparison. His sheer size turned her on despite his amateur performance. Actually, she realized, he probably thought that he was doing a better job than he actually was because she was getting off on his love hammer.

Love hammer was one of Sara's terms and it made Kelly snicker every time it was used. She couldn't wait to tell her about the size of this `love hammer'.

She could only deep throat him to about half his length and that took work. Her tongue flickered everything that could get to as she bobbed up and down. It was hurting her jaw a bit, so she had to stop to rest. At the other end, his slurping was at least keeping the status quo.

"Suck me baby," he said.

She let spit fall from her month onto his penis. The lubrication should make it a little easier to suck. This time she sucked from the side, up and down as her right hand massaged the parts that she couldn't swallow. He liked that. After a few minutes, she decided that it was time to take it to the next stage.

Reaching into her drawer, she pulled out a large condom and put it onto him. "This is the biggest that I have," she said. "I hope that it fits."

He made a face, pretending that it was too tight. Actually, it was more than a

little snug and he had to help her get it on. He looked pleased with himself as he laid back waiting for her.

Lowering slowly she gradually took him in. Dear god, she thought. It's stretching me.

There was a little pain and a whole lot of pleasure. However, she admitted that a large portion of the pleasure came from the novelty of having such a monster inside of her that hung from such a perfect looking man. She looked down at what laid naked in her bed.

Christ! She thought. He is so f'ing gorgeous.

She let out a little scream when she had him in to her limit. Unfortunately, he wasn't completely in and she was still in the air so she couldn't rub her clitoris against his pelvis. However, plan B wasn't so bad. Slowly she rode up and down on his penis, taking as much of him as she could. After a dozen strokes, she shifted to the squatting position and was able to ride a little quicker by not having to take as much of him in. He seemed to like that and shouted his approval, "Oh go baby, ride my giant love toy. Oh god, ride. God, you're a lovely piece of ass!

She got into quite the rhythm that was doing wonders for her and was lost in another world, far away from his juvenile comments. As he got closer to cumming, he added, "Fuck me pussy! Ride that thing. God, you can fuck bitch! Come on pussy. Fuck! Fuck! Fuck!"

The force of his explosion hit the tip and the sides of the condom so much that she felt it. She came again soon after and stopped the ride.

"Fantastic," he shouted.

She gently rose to let him fall out of her. She felt satisfied and a little sore. Both of them were sweaty and as he laid there trying to cool down he said to no one in particular, "What a nice tight pussy."

She raised an eyebrow. "Ah thanks."

"You certainly know how to handle a big dick. Most women don't know what to do with it."

"I've had experience with big dicks." She glared at him. He didn't pick up on the double entendre.

He looked hurt. "You've had bigger than me?"

"No, I think that you're the biggest dick that I've come across." The cutting remark was lost on him as he took it as a compliment.

She thought that with a little molding, he could be less irritating and control

lable. After all, he wasn't too bright. She could quite easily hammer him into the man that she wanted. However, the more that she thought about it, the more that the truth rang out. She concluded that he really is a bad lover. That fact had been clouded all along by how gorgeous he is and how massive his penis is.

He got up and started looking for his clothes. She admired his strong muscular legs, nice butt and strong back. "You don't have to go," she said.

He didn't look at her when he said, "Sorry girl, but it is a policy of mine to only fuck a woman once. Sorry but that is the way it is." He found his clothes then in an effort to be nice said, "I tell you what, you can have my underwear as an souvenir."

Stunned, she didn't say a word nor did she move until she heard him say, "Bye." When she heard the door closed, she locked it behind him.

In her 'Dicksinary' she wrote that she had been with the most arrogant man that she had ever met. Still, she had good things to say about his size and looks. His technique scored very low which, considering that he probably saw himself as the world's greatest lover, was pretty ironic.

She closed the book, put it away then went off to bed. Oh my god, she was sore and that killed any idea of going out to find someone else, someone who actually knew what they were doing.

She got underneath the covers and hated herself.

Look at me, she thought as she stared at the ceiling. I can get a great guy who is lousy in bed and I can get a beautiful guy who is a total jerk. Why can't I find someone who is both of these? Or at least a good balance of both.

She sighed and thought, I can probably get a total jerk that was lousy in bed. She laughed. Actually, I've had a few of those; too many.

She knew that the domino effect had been playing havoc with her. Since she pushed Doug away, she had been pushed into getting it on with someone who that she wouldn't normally have been with and that has left her feeling like shit. Maybe Doug paid this guy to do this to me, she mused. No, she concluded, he wouldn't do that.

Her apartment was quiet. Occasionally, she heard a car drive up, some people talk and then a door slam. She tried to think of the positive. She liked her job, her family (for the most part), her apartment and her friends. The only thing that she didn't like was this string of losers lately. She hoped that her luck would change.

Of course, she wouldn't mind having someone more steady, someone who

she could see on a regular basis who wouldn't criticize her lifestyle and/or treat her like crap. Needless to say, actor-boy had taken his toll on her. He was a heartbreaker of the worst kind. He had ruined even a one-night stand, and that is hard to do with Kelly.

ALONE

Kelly tried not to think of Mr. No Brains/Ego Boy, but she had to admit that – as annoying as he was – it was quite the thrill ride, something to do once. Physically he was a perfect man. Even though it wasn't all that pleasurable and there were times that she almost stopped, there was something about last night's conquest that peaked her interest. On the sex scale it was a four, but on the scale of adventure, it was a ten. Most of the time she didn't know what was going to happen next or even if they were going to do it at all. Who knew what was going to happen?

Was that it, she wondered? Was it the thrill of the unknown that has gotten me going? It certainly wasn't that jerk. There were moments that he was actually turning me off.

It took her awhile to conclude that one of the things that turned her on was that she was in control of the situation. It was after Mr. No Brains gave into her ultimatum that she got really turned on. From that point on he was too afraid to move or say any-thing in fear of being sent home with no dessert. Then again, just having him shut-up would have had the same effect. One of Sara's favorite sayings about guys like that came to mind: "He was great looking until he opened his mouth."

One thing is for sure; she really didn't need to hear his farewell remark. How degrading. He became an all-star jerk with that one, possibly captain of the all-star jerk team.

Sunday she visited her mother and it was the perfect distraction to forget things. Most of the conversation was about her sister and her kids and their problems. Kelly listened and was glad that the focus wasn't on her messed up life. Monday morning she took on a new client and that allowed her to get into her work. However, by Wednesday she was in the mood to get naked with someone again. She was going to call one of her regulars – god she hated how that made her sound like a hooker – when she got home, but there was already a message waiting for her. She hit the play button.

"Hey it's Steve," a low voice said, a voice from her not so distant past. "I'm just wondering how you are and what has been happening with you. Give me a call when you can. Bye."

"Hmmm...someone wants to get laid," she said. She liked the idea of that. "Hey that works for me."

Not bothering to play games, she looked up his number in her `Dicksinary' and called him. As she listened to the rings she reread her notes on him from last October with addendum from November, December and January. It said, "Above average in size and technique. Looks okay to good. Certainly do if the time and place is convenient."

"Hi Kelly," Steve said. "Just get in from work?"

"Yep just I got your message. It's been awhile. What three months?"

"Closer to four, I think. Way too long. What have you been doing all this time?"

"Nothing too different. Was seeing this guy for awhile, but things didn't work out."

"Oh that's too bad." He didn't sound too disappointed for her.

"Hey, shit happens. What's up with you?"

"Um." His tone changed. "I have a question for you and I hope that I don't offend you…"

"Okay…"

"Now promise me that you won't take offense, okay?"

"Yeah, sure. You know me, you can ask anything, but if I don't want to do it, I'll say no and that's that."

He chuckled. "That's what I love about you,

straight to the point. No b.s."

"As long as I don't get jerked around." Memory of actor-boy made her shutter, but she knew that Steve was not like that.

"Of course."

"So what is your question?" Her curiosity was peaked.

"Um, maybe I should ask you in person. Are you free tomorrow night for a drink?"

"Steve! Don't do that. Ask me now."

He sighed, then said, "Okay, no offense, but…"

"Get on with it!"

"Okay. I've been seeing this girl for the last four months and…"

"That's why you haven't called lately," she interjected.

"Ah, yeah…"

"That's cool. No problem."

"Good." He took a deep breath. "And I've talked her into trying a threesome. She said she would if we could find the right person. Naturally, I thought of you. I know that you have been with a woman before – so you're not opposed to the idea of being naked with another girl – and that you're pretty adventurous. So is this something that you would consider?"

She was a little stunned. No, she wasn't opposed to the idea of having a threesome. However, it would be new for her.

Silence.

"Kelly?"

"I'm thinking."

"Have I offended you."

"Oh god no. In fact, I'm flattered. Um, what's she like? You know that I used to screw you at the drop of a hat and probably still would…"

"Thank you."

"But I haven't said yes yet. I'm still considering it. I have to meet her first before I decide to get naked with her. You know that my experience with women is limited."

"Yes, but you have had experience and you do like them, right?"

"Yes, I guess so."

"Now there is one catch."

"What I have to pay you?" She laughed at her own

joke.

He laughed too, and then added wryly, "Now there's an idea."

She didn't expect the phone to ring so soon after she had just hung up. It was John, another `regular'. "How you've been?" He asked.

"Good. You?"

"The same."

"Why don't you pop over."

"Hmm...now there's a good idea. Now?"

"Sure. I have to take a shower, but I'll leave the door unlocked. Just come on in."

"Into the shower?"

She giggled, "sure. Why not?"

"Be right over."

She unlocked the door and started to disrobe as she walked towards the shower. She figured that if he hurried he could be over in five minutes and she knew that since his time was always limited he would hurry. The quicker he came and went, the less chance of his wife finding out about it. He sometimes complained of how she kept on strict eye on him to which she quipped, "I can't imagine why she would do that?"

In the shower she closed her eyes as she softly rubbed the soap over her body. God I'm turned on, she thought. I have a man coming over to help me shower.

She almost came when she cleaned her undercarriage. Her nipples grew when she heard the door open, close then lock. Her breathing intensified as someone approached. The thought that it could be a rapist or a murder crossed her mind and she thought as hot as having a quickie with John in the shower was maybe it wasn't such a good idea to leave the door unlocked. The bathroom door opened and closed. Someone was inside. She resisted saying anything. Instead, she leaned against the wall in anticipation, the water cascading down her svelte body.

The shower curtain opened slowly and a naked well-built man stood on the other side. The handsome man eyes brightened as they took in the sight of Kelly's naked wet body. His penis grew and by the time that he had gotten into the shower and within reach of Kelly's hands it was fully erect. He kissed her and admired her body with her hands. She squirmed with every touch and loudly moaned when he slipped a finger into her pussy.

"God, you are so wet," he said.

"Yes. Oddly enough that happens in a shower."

He chuckled. "No, I meant sexually."

All in one motion, he dropped to his knees lifted her up, spread her legs and gave her pussy one giant long lick from bottom to top. How she didn't cum immediately she didn't know. His tongue was busy and intense. It drove her wild. A dozen licks later she came hard, but he didn't stop, even after a protest or two. She was practically in tears with his tortuous assault on her sensitive bits. He didn't stop until she came again.

"Hmmm nice," he said. She didn't know, but she had squirted directly into his mouth. He stopped and licked his lips.

He quickly mounted her against the wall, but sometime during one of her organism he had managed to apply a condom. Now that is my type of multi-tasking, she thought.

He rode her hard and she clung onto him with both her legs and arms wrapped around his strong body. She enjoyed the sensation that his penis was creating and it speeded in and out of her. She hung on and concentrated on the feeling. It built as he got quicker and quicker, finally topping out at his top speed. At that pace it didn't take him long to come and that was okay with her.

She was satisfied several orgasms ago

"Thank you," she said softly

"Until next time."

He kissed her goodbye then got dressed and left. She happily finished her shower.

Friday night she decided to go home to veg in front of the TV. This she did gladly. She felt strangely contented. Then again, she always did for days after a session with John. He was that good. Not the best-looking guy around, but he knew the female anatomy. Sometimes she thought that it was too bad that he was married.

Other times when common sense kicked in she was glad that he was married. As good as they were in bed together they weren't compatible in life, too many different ideas on...well, everything from religion to which wine to drink. John's role in her life was to be an occasional fuck buddy. He was a part-time tool or P.T.T. Nothing more. Nothing less. She actually hoped that his wife never found out about her. That would wreak the arrangement. Or worse, she would leave him and then he would then want to change the one that she had with her.

Speaking of arrangements, she thought of what Steve and her had worked out. It was a simple plan and she thought that those always had the best chances of being successful. The plan was this, Steve and Gail would be at the Pussy Pub around eight on Saturday. Kelly was to `bump' into Steve, pretending to be an old friend from work. They would share a drink and if Kelly was interested she would put the moves on Gail, who was unaware of what was happening. She had said that she would do a girl under the right circumstances. Of course, Steve was trying to create just that.

Kelly got there early so that she could throw a few back before she had to meet anyone. She needed her old ally, beer to do this. Sara had tagged along partly out of curiosity, but mostly to have an excuse to get out of the house for the evening. "We don't hang out like we used to," she told Kelly.

"I do. It's you that's gone off and gotten married. I hang out alone these days."

"I know. Life is good, but sometimes I miss the old lifestyle. Freedom. Total freedom.

"A little bored are we?"

"No, no. God no. I'm just missing the old days a

bit. I won't trade my marriage for it. The old days weren't all roses."

"That's true."

Kelly had picked a table at the back of the Pussy Pub so she could see Steve and his girlfriend enter. They did almost right on time. He held the door open for `her'.

"Oh my," Kelly gasped.

"Is that them who just walked in?" Sara asked.

"Yes."

"Her boobs are huge."

"No kidding." She pondered the situation. "I need a few more beers."

"You need a keg! Look at the size of them. They can't be real. Her hips are too thin."

"No, they're not real. He warned me about the size of them."

Sara stared at Kelly as expecting an answer. "Well?"

"Well what?"

"You know?" She gave her a look and motioned with her head toward the walking boobs on a stick.

"I have to see what she is like first."

"Well, one thing is for sure. It is a good thing that you're so thin because there won't be much room left in the bed once she's gotten those things into one."

"Ha...funny."

The couple made their way to an empty spot at the end of the bar. All the tables were full, another reason why Kelly got there early. As the couple got close enough, Kelly said, "Is that Steve Jones?"

"Oh...hi Kelly," he said. "How long has it been?" He won't have won an academy award for his acting, but it was good enough in a noisy crowded bar. "This is my girlfriend, Gail."

Up close Gail's face was sweet. She was cute and innocent looking, the total opposite of Kelly's sultry bedroom eyes gaze. Kelly wished that she looked like Gail, cute face, slim waist and over-sized breasts. Kelly introduced her friend and invited the couple to sit with them at their table. Steve accepted and offered to buy a round of drinks.

Kelly was glad that they quickly got through the cover story and onto something else. Gail started talking about how she and Steve had met. It turned out that according to Kelly's math, Steve was still popping over to her house for a quickie as he started to date Gail. He must have been banging me until she put out, she thought. Interesting. At least, he had the decency to stop once they were a couple.

She didn't want to think of the fact that she was passed over for someone who was better looking and was girlfriend material. Instead, she blamed the fact that she was an island that only could be visited at certain times and only for so long. And besides, she would have never given Steve permission to live on her island. He could only vacation there.

Even though she could appreciate how attractive Gail was she wasn't sure if she was attracted to her or not. She decided to play the 'wait and see card'. It was exciting because she knew that Steve was trying to read reaction from not only her, but from Sara as well. Clearly, he hadn't expected to see her there and he wasn't quite sure what was going to happen or not. Even more exciting to Kelly was the fact that with so many variables thrown into this equation, anything could happen.

"Where do you work?" Kelly asked Gail. She figured that she could at least find out who this chick was and where she was coming from.

"I work in cosmetics."

"Oh what company?"

"Sears."

"So sales then."

"Yes, My booth is...

A simple sales girl, she thought as she listened to her talk about her job. That would explain the princess mannerisms.

Soon the conversation switched to Kelly and Sara's jobs. Gail seemed to be impressed with their good work of helping abused women.

"Well, it certainly can be rewarding at times, but sometimes the guy isn't as evil as the woman claims he is. Nor is the woman the woman as hard done by as they want us to believe. Sometimes they just want to bleed the guy of everything he has all for the simple reason that he left."

"Really?

"Every case is different and most times it is just sad. Nobody wins. Everyone loses."

"Still, it is good work. All I do is help woman smell better. When I have a bad day, I stink up the world a little."

Kelly laughed because she knew that this was this girl's idea of a joke. Still she

liked her and her humble attitude. She was a simple girl who didn't try to be anything more than that. Well, no more than a simple well-stacked girl. She should wear a nametag that states: Hello, my name is Gail and these are my personalities.

Sara noticed Kelly's look of approval and decided that it was time to go. She looked at her watch and said. "I told my husband that I would be back before ten."

Steve was clearly disappointed and Kelly suppressed laughing at him. Obviously his imagination had been working over time and he had already added Sara to the mix.

"Oh that's too bad." Gail said. "It was very nice meeting you."

Before she left Sara whispered into Kelly's ear. "I'm living vicariously through you now. Go for it."

After she left, Steve started to complain about the high price of beer and suggested that they go back to his place for a drink. Kelly said that she didn't have a problem with changing locations, but Gail didn't want to leave quite yet. "We only just got here," she said. Neither Kelly nor Steve bothered to argue with her. They ordered another round.

Kelly decided that Gail wasn't someone who she could hate and wasn't one of those attention demanding prima donnas that thought that their shit didn't stink. Because of this Kelly allowed herself to warm up to this woman both as a person and physically. She couldn't help look at and admire Gail's large breasts. Yes, she liked them and now that she had accepted her she was becoming physically very attracted to her. It was women like Gail that reminded Kelly that she was bisexual. It didn't take Gail very long before she realized that she was being lusted over by another woman, Kelly's bedroom eyes had now kicked in. At first she was a little uneasy with that.

"Do you have a boyfriend?" Gail asked her.

"No need for one," she said and let Gail interpret that how she wanted to.

"You do like men, right?"

"Oh, of course I do. Actually, I just broke up with Doug a little while ago."

"Oh, good." There was an awkward pause before Gail added, "I mean not that you broke up but that you like men." She was stumbling.

"Why? Do you have a problem with lesbians?"

"Oh no, of course not. I…"

"Do they make you nervous?"

"Some do."

"Why?"

"Because they hit on me and try to make me hate men. I like men and I don't know why they…"

Kelly listened to Gail's nervous rant and only smiled. The woman was uneasy with Kelly's presence and this gave Kelly a lift. She had an effect on her. Kelly watched Gail's chest move with her breathing. Kelly's own breathing had intensified and her heart was beating quicker. She wasn't sure where this was going, but it certainly was entertaining. She upped the ante. "I can see why they hit on you, you're very beautiful."

Steve agreed. Gail blushed and took a drink. Then she took another one. Kelly and Steve looked at each other and smiled. There was innocence to Gail that they both were enjoyed. It was like watching a virgin hearing the details of sex for the first time. "What goes where?"

In order to ease Gail, Kelly said, "Don't worry, I only date men."

She nodded. Gail looked seriously at Kelly. "Can I

ask you a question?"

"Sure."

"How you ever been with a woman?"

"Of course I have, haven't you?" She gave her a look like everyone has done it, why haven't you. This pleased Steve who surreptitiously gave her the thumbs up.

Gail shook her head. Weakly she said, "no."

"Does the idea excite or repulse you? Ever have a fantasy about another woman?"

Gail looked around to see if anyone at the other tables was listening. There were too many people around.

"You have haven't you," Kelly said playfully. "Don't worry we all have. It is very natural."

"I'm not comfortable talking about it here."

That was Steve's cue. He said, "Good, let's go back to my place. I have plenty of beer and we can talk without anyone overhearing."

Kelly had never been to Steve's place and when she walked in, she wasn't sorry that they always got together at her place. It was obvious that interior decorating wasn't his forte. Well, he likes hockey, she thought as looked at his choice of art. A picture of the final game at the Maple Leaf Gardens was his piece de resistance.

Gail sat at one of the couch and Kelly sat at the other end. Steve went to get the drinks.

"There is nothing to be ashamed about you know," Kelly said.

"I know. It's just that I don't want anyone to know. It's private."

"Yes. It's very intimate." She spoke very deliberately and peered into Gail's eyes. "Being with a woman or even just thinking of pleasing another woman is very sensuous."

"I can imagine that things would be softer and gentler."

"Very!" Kelly peered directly into her eyes. Her bedroom were now awake.

Gail stared back. "You have beautiful blue eyes," she said. "They're so full of...life."

Steve came back with the drinks and placed them on the coffee table. He tried to sit between the girls, but Gail told him to go and sit on the chair. "Kelly and I have things to talk about," she said. "If you're good then you can listen. And by good, I mean silent."

Sheepishly, he obeyed and watched with interest from the chair. From this point on he was to be a fly on the wall.

"Kelly," Gail said softly. She stared directly into Kelly's eyes, totally ignoring her boyfriend.

"Yes." Kelly let her eyes wander, first to her breasts then to her slim waist.

There was a slight pause before Gail said nervously, "Do you like me?"

"Yes, I do." Kelly smiled.

"In that way?"

"Yes, in that way."

Gail smiled. "Can you teach me what to do with another woman?"

Kelly leaned forward and softly kissed Gail on the cheek. Gail closed her eyes and waited for another kiss. Unexpectantly, it came on her lips. It didn't take much for Gail to start kissing back. Tongues intertwined between the soft sliding of lips.

"Oh wow," Steve said. His fly on the wall role was ignored.

Rachel Richards

Kelly's hands found Gail's breasts and massaged them. She wanted to suck them so she broke off the kiss.

"Your lips are so soft," Gail said.

"So is the rest of me," Kelly said. "Touch me." Gail's hand caressed the parts of Kelly's body that she could reach as Kelly lifted Gail's blouse and lowered her lips to the exposed part of her breasts. To her, the bra looked like it was overworked so she reached behind and unclasped it to give it the night off.

"Allow me," Gail said and she slid her bra off. She then shoved her breasts into Kelly's face. Kelly's face disappeared into the oversized mounds of flesh. She was really enjoying herself now. One thing that she came to realize was that when it came to woman she was a breast man, err... woman. She liked them large. She figured that because opposites attract her lack of cup size made her admire any woman with a nice rack. Secretly, she wished that hers were like Gail's, big and soft. Sometimes, she also wished that she had a penis, but that is a totally different subject. Actually, she wished she had one right now. She could see why men love to ride woman like Gail. She wanted to drive her wild.

And she did. After admiring her breasts for some time, Kelly went down on Gail. With both hands she gently pulled Gail's lips apart then used her tongue to explore the area between them. Gail's moans told her where the sensitive spots were and it wasn't long before Gail came.

Kelly leaned against the couch and waited for Gail's eyes to reopen. When they did, she said "Now do the same to me."

Gail helped Kelly out of her blouse and bra. Gail kissed a tit repeatedly and then licked the nipple. "That's it," Kelly said. "Do to them what you like having done to yours."

Gail sucked on a nipple and gently massaged the tit. Kelly liked that and told her so.

Kelly unbuttoned her pants and Gail watched as she slid them off. "Keeping going," Gail said. She sounded like she was enjoying the striptease. Kelly slid off her panties and let them dangle across Gail's breasts. While staring intensely at Gail, she dropped them on the floor, leaned back, spread her legs and mouthed the words, "Eat me."

Reluctantly at first, Gail kissed Kelly's inner thigh and worked her way to Kelly's pussy. She was a little taken back by the smell of it. Kelly knew this and said, "It's strong because I'm really wet."

Kelly looked over to see Steve lick his lips. Her's was a smell that he knew well.

Gail kissed the vagina then kissed it again at a different spot. Her soft lips felt good to Kelly. With her hands, Kelly spread her lips for the woman. "Lick me," she said. Gail obeyed and gave into the spirit of it. Occasionally, Kelly gave her a suggestion, but for the most part Kelly sat back and enjoyed being the woman's first experience.

By this time, Steve was already naked and was positioning Gail to take her from behind, doggy style. Kelly's and his eyes met and they both smiled. He rammed his penis home and Gail yelped. Much to her disappointment, Gail stopped licking her as Steve rode her like a demon. He was incredibly turned on and Kelly watched him with amusement. He can't last, she thought and she was right.

After he had finished and pulled out, Gail said, "Now where were we?"

"You were sweetly eating my pussy," Kelly said.

"Oh right."

Gail's tongue flickered Kelly's clitoris and a finger slid into her. She was enjoying this, but suggested, "Use two fingers." Gail looked at her, obeyed and with her fingers she started searching. She knew that she found what she was looking for when Kelly gasped.

"There we are," Gail said. Then with a come hither motion she teased Kelly's G-spot.

"Jesus-fucking-Christ that's good!" Kelly yelled.

Relentlessly, Gail kept up that attack until Kelly arched her back, shouted to god and lubricated Gail's fingers with her cum.

"Christ I've never seen you cum like that," Steve said. Then realized what he had said.

Gail stopped. "What?"

"I'm mean you," he said pointing to Gail.

"Well maybe you should learn to do that," Gail said.

Humbly, he nodded. "Yes."

Kelly had fallen back onto the couch and looked like she had been shot. Gail softly kissed her lips and caressed her face. "Kelly," Gail said. "Are you okay?"

Kelly wrapped her hands around Gail's head, drew her close and gave her a huge kiss. "That was totally wonderful," she said. "Where did you learn to that?"

Gail giggled. "Oh did you actually believe me when I said that I've never been with another woman?"

Kelly shouted, "Ha! We've been doped."

"I like being seduced and `taught'. It's fun being pursued and you seem to like being in control so I let you."

Steve seemed puzzled. "Why then didn't you tell me that you've been with another woman? Why the big act? We could have just gone out and picked up someone."

She looked at him. "Well, I wanted to check out one of your old girlfriends."

Steve's mouth dropped open and Kelly clapped her hands. "Busted!" She said.

"Oh I knew who you were exactly when we `bumped' into each other. By the way Steve was rushing me out the door and acting I knew that it was a set-up. What I didn't know was if it was you or Sara."

"Are you disappointed that it wasn't Sara?"

"Sara's cute, but I like natural redheads with a passion for have sexing."

"That's me."

"So how long did you two date?"

Kelly told her how they had a one-night stand then he would pop over for sex until he had gotten a girlfriend. This didn't win him any points with Gail who said, "So, you used this nice girl for sex then ignored her until you wanted her again." She cuddled Kelly by pulling Kelly's face into her breasts and stroked her head. "Oh you poor thing." Kelly soaked up the warmth and softness.

"It's okay," Kelly said. "I didn't mind."

"Men are jerks."

"Yes men are evil. Hold me." She smirked. She had tried to say that with a straight face, but couldn't. After she stopped she said, "The only good thing about men are their dicks and only when they're hard."

"Yes, I concur." Then turning to Steve she commanded, "Steve."

"Yes?"

"Get an erection now. You're going to screw this poor girl and you're going to do it right."

Kelly smiled.

With her head still buried in Gail's titanic breasts, Steve slid in and out of Kelly's pussy. Her face was caressed by the softness of Gail's hand while the top of her head received soft kisses.

This woman is making love to me as her boyfriend is fucking me, she thought. Who the hell is this woman?

Kelly never wanted this to end. She looked up at Gail who was looking down, admiring her. Their eyes met and she felt a connection with her that was deeper than she had felt in a long time. She melted as Steve's penis raced in and out of her.

"Oh god," Steve shouted. His body language told everyone that he was cumming.

He collapsed onto the couch and Gail commented, "Oh twice in one night, he's done."

"Yep."

"He'll be asleep soon."

Kelly softly kissed Gail on the lips. "Thank you."

"You're very welcome."

Gail's arms pushed Kelly closer so she could kiss her. Their lips met and Kelly lost herself in the softness of her lips. Her hands gently caressed Gail's breasts while Gail caressed her ass. Kelly stopped kissing long enough to moan then reacquired Gail's lips to attack them with even more passion. After a few minutes, Gail broke it off. They stared into each other's eyes.

"I should go home," Kelly said.

"Okay." A juxtaposition of expressions crossed Gail's face. She looked both sad and relieved. "Let me drive you home."

"Thank you."

Kelly got up and started to dress. She tried to maintain control over her emotions and excused herself to go to the washroom. Inside the bathroom, she closed her eyes and took several deep breaths. She told herself that everything was okay. Truth was she was more than a little freaked out by how close she felt to another woman. She knew that she didn't want to fall in love with a woman.

Kel, she yelled at herself, don't think about this until you get home. Think about anything else but…

Both Steve and Gail were dressed by the time she came back to the living room.

"Ready?" Gail said.

"Yes," she said brightly.

"That was amazing," Steve said.

"I had fun."

"You always do." He kissed Kelly goodbye.

"I'll call you tomorrow Steve," Gail said.

Kelly walked out the door to give them a minute or two alone. She waited by the elevator. She heard a door close and Gail was walking towards her.

"Man," Gail said. "He is beat."

"I know. Usually one shot and he's done. Twice will put him in a coma."

Gail laughed. "Oh I know. No endurance."

Kelly said wryly, "Single shot Steve."

Gail howled and was still laughing when they reached her car. She opened the Escort's passenger door for Kelly and held it open for her.

"What a gentleman," Kelly said.

"Well, if I'm going to start sleeping with women I might as well start acting like a gentlemen. It will get me laid more."

Kelly laughed nervously and got in. She got a couple of good deep breaths in before Gail walked around and got in the driver's seat. It didn't surprise her that Gail leaned over to kiss her. Kelly kissed her back.

Gail broke it off and as her hand caressed Kelly's

cheek she said, "Thank you for being such a sport."

"You're welcome. I had a great time."

"I know you did."

Kelly smiled.

After another kiss, Gail sat back in the driver's seat and started the car. "Where do you live?"

Kelly told her and Gail made small talk as she drove. This eased Kelly until Gail pulled in front of her apartment.

"Maybe next time you can stay over," Gail said. "We'll plan it for a weekend."

"That would be good," she said.

"Kelly!"

Yes?"

"I really want there to be a next time."

Kelly stared at the woman and knew that there would be a next time. The goodnight kiss was long and very tender, something that Kelly had been missing for a while. This both excited her and scared the hell out of her.

QUICK AND EASY

Maybe I should have taken Steve and Gail up on their offer and stayed over, she thought. Even with the hassle of getting up in the morning it might have been better. No, I'm glad that I left. I screw them, and then leave and I certainly don't fall in love with a woman. Gail was great, but she's just a plaything.

This kind of contradiction plagued Kelly's thoughts.

Even though she was determined not to let it go any further, she knew that Gail had touched her more than physically. She thought that it was just the

tenderness of another woman that did it, but she had been with other woman before without feeling like this. This bothered her. Still, she knew that tonight was different somehow and she wanted to know why, knowing full well that sleep wouldn't come until she figured it out. As she got ready for bed, she wondered why she enjoyed the evening so much. Yes, the sex was really good, but there was something more. It took her a few minutes to realize that for most of the night she held the power, she was in charge. That excited her! Even with John's 'visits' she still was in charge. It was her who decided when the door was unlocked.

So do I need to be the driver? She thought. And having a submissive person like Gail did it for me. Controlling Steve was a turn on as well. She smiled at the way she had controlled him. No Steve. Wait. Okay, now Steve you can join in.

Having come to grips with the fact that she likes being in control she felt freer, more at ease with herself. Now all she wanted to do was to go on another adventure to test the theory. Lying in bed, she pictured herself going up to a good-looking guy and without saying a word, taking his hand to lead him to a back room. She would push him onto a desk and undo his pants. He of course would be smiling and by the time that she got his pants and underwear off, he would be hard as a rock. With both hands jerking his shaft, he sucked on his penis, lapping her tongue all over the head, soaking it with her saliva. She would bring him to the point of cumming then stop. He would protest, but she wouldn't care. She was in control and if he wanted more then he would have to play by her rules.

She didn't remember exactly when she started touching herself, she only knew that she had a great fantasy going and she was on her way to cumming. Pausing only long enough to retrieve her vibrator from the night table and to turn it on, she was back into the fantasy. As she slid the fake dick into her vagina she pictured herself lowering onto his nice hard penis. With every stroke she rode in her dream, the vibrator matched. Reality and fantasy became blurred as she tossed her head back and forth to the rhythm of the motorized dildo's flight path. In and out at a quick pace her right hand worked as her the index finger on her left hand flickered her clitoris. She pictured an image, though slightly unrealistic, and it did the trick. She was getting off, soaking the guy's dick and public hairs with her cum and forcing another woman to lick it up.

After she was finished, she wondered how much sex a person can have. I'm out of control, she thought. And loving it!

Satisfied for now, she felt off to sleep.

She woke up the next day with the same opinion about herself; she got off on control and was anxious to prove this theory. So when she found out that the girls said that they wanted to go for drinks after work on Wednesday for Debbie's birthday, she was all for it. I'm in the market for some meat that I can beat, she thought. Some lucky guy will be only too glad that I will use him just for sex and he doesn't have to do a damn thing but like it.

Debbie was the talker of the group or as Sara and Kelly called her behind her back, the loud mouth. She was going on about her new boyfriend when they walked into the bar and was still rambling long after they were seated. However, Kelly didn't mind Debbie's motor mouth, listening to nothing took the pressure of her having to really listen and it allowed herself to look around.

The first thing she noticed was that this place was filled with suits and skirts, quite the different from the clientele where she usually hangs out. To her surprise, and she did a double take to make sure, one of them was Matt's friend. She spotted him sitting with several guys, all dressed in suits and looking very corporate. He either pretended not to see her when they made eye contact or it didn't register.

I must tell Matt that I keep seeing his boyfriend everywhere, she thought, and with other men. Uh-oh, maybe he wouldn't like hearing that?

She was drawn back to conversation when she heard Sara ask Debbie, "Have you slept with him yet?"

"Sara!" Linda said, shocked with the question.

"If I can ask?" Sara added, smiling at Debbie.

"It's okay Lyn," Debbie said. "I don't mind the question. In fact, I was going

to ask round the table when the best time to give in."

"On you're wedding night," Linda said automatically.

Kelly briefly wondered why Linda was even here, but she remembered that she knew the answer to that. Debbie and her were pretty tight, a fact that seemed to be puzzling.

After a group sigh, Debbie said, "Now that the religious right has been heard from, let's here from..." she looked around the table. "Sara. When you were still on the manhunt..."

"After a couple of dates," Sara said, "if I thought that it was going somewhere."

"Jill?"

"Two months minimal," Jill said.

This was met with more than a few gasps, most of them from Kelly and Sara. Kelly didn't want to add to this conversation, in fact she wanted to avoid answering if possible, but the gasp just came out. This was not unnoticed by Debbie.

"Okay, Kel," Debbie said, "what is your timetable?"

"Yes girl, how long do you wait?" Sara mocked.

Kelly gave her a dirty look. Fortunately, the waitress came to take the orders. "I'll take a Bud," she said, evading the question.

"And an American, a Brit, a Frenchman and just about anyone else," Sara joked.

"Very funny." She tried to angrily peer at her friend, but she couldn't hold it. Soon she was laughing.

After the waitress had gone, Debbie readdressed the question.

Since Kelly knew that her co-worker won't let her off the hook that easy, she had time to prepare an answer.

"It depends," she said. "Every situation is different. Sometimes, it is good to wait, while other times it is good that things happen right away."

Both Sara and Jill broke couldn't suppress their giggles. Jill managed to say, "By waiting, she means by finishing her beer first."

"Or finding out the guy's name," Sara added.

Kelly was a little embarrassed by the comments, but on the surface she managed to laugh along with the others.

"Very funny," Kelly said. "I'm not that bad."

"Funny and true, me thinks," Debbie said.

"No!"

"How long did you wait with your last boyfriend?"

Jill said, "Oh come on, she at least finished her dinner, watched an entire movie before jumping him."

Kelly didn't laugh along with the others. Am I that bad? She hoped not.

"It's okay Kel," Sara said. "You are who you are and it could be worse."

"Ah, how?"

"You could be frigid like Linda here," Sara said.

Linda was clearly offended by this, which cancelled out any offence that Kelly had felt earlier. "I won't get into any details, but Lawrence and I have a good sex life, thank-you-very-much! Good things happen when you wait."

"But until marriage, no thank you. You think that it is good because you have nothing to compare it with."

"Well, isn't that better?" Linda said.

"Ladies!" Debbie interrupted, "Getting back to my original question…"

"I really like sex," Kelly said. "And I wouldn't be stuck with someone who doesn't know what they're doing…so…sex happens quickly with me."

"And when was your last long time relationship," Linda asked. She didn't bother to hide her condescending tone

"When I last wanted one."

"And why don't you want a boyfriend? Afraid to commit?"

"Not to a jerk, or to someone who is unworthy. When I met someone of quality, then I will give it a go. Again."

"You won't trap someone of quality by giving it up so quickly."

"But I don't want to `trap' anyone. If they want to be with me then I shouldn't have to use sex as a weapon. Nor do I want to deny myself of pleasure in fear of him not calling me again."

"That's fair enough," Debbie said, feeling like the UN throwing themselves between two warring fractions in order to keep the peace, she quickly changed the subject.

Unknown the Kelly, but their conversation had been overheard by a few people at the adjoining tables who were more than a little intrigued by Kelly's attitudes. One of them was a thirty-two year old Architect, named Jim who made it a point to make sure that Kelly knew that he was checking her out. He was average height and build with dark hair and strong facial features. She figured that his background was Greek or someplace in the Mediterranean.

He continued to be interested but waited patiently for an opportunity. Kelly enjoyed keeping him at bay while the girls had a few more drinks. During this time, she also kept on eye on Matt's friend who seemed to be pretty occupied. She entertained the thought of going over and forcing herself on him. It would certainly prove if he was gay or not.

Linda was the first to leave, followed shortly by Debbie and Jill.

That only left Sara alone with Kelly. "It looks like

you might be going upscale tonight," Sara said. "He is interested in you."

"If something happens I will tell you all about it."

"What happened to your quest for a L.I.T?"

"Well, I'm still on it – despite my recent adventures – and this might be part of it."

"I hope so."

"Me too" Kelly said. "Live and learn." She wished that she could find someone who could help her sort out who she really was.

Sara left for the bathroom and Jim wasted no time. He was chatting Kelly up even before Sara had cleared the room. "I've never seen you here before," he said. "Are you new to the area?"

"Sort of. I work close by."

"Really? Where do you work?"

"Close." She looked at her glass. "My drink is empty."

"Allow me to I buy you another one."

She tried to figure him out, but kept wondering what his penis looked and tasted like. Oh well, she figured that old habits did hard. He looked good. "Sure."

When Sara came back, they chatted only long enough for Sara to get a feel for this guy. "He's a player," she whispered when he went for another round. "And kind of full of himself."

"I think that to," Kelly said, "but I don't mind. He's hot. Maybe I should play him. Show him who really is in control."

"So much for the quest," she said sadly. "Oh well."

"Just be careful, okay pervert? There's something about him that I don't like. I'm not sure what though."

"I'll keep that in mind. Here's his business card. Keep it as insurance, you know if something does happen." Sara knew that this guy knew that Sara knew exactly who he was and that he had better treat her well. Even if the name on the card was fake, it still contained his fingers and DNA. More than enough evidence for the police."

"You watch too much C.S.I."

"True."

Sara left and it was another round before Jim asked Kelly if she wanted to see the view from his new condo. "Love to," she said.

His place did indeed have quite the view of the

harbour. She looked out as he watched her from behind. She didn't know it, but as she was admiring the view he was admiring a different view: her ass. He came up from behind and hugged her. She unclasped his hands and walked away.

"Can I have a drink," she said. She didn't really want one, but she wanted to obtain control of the situation.

He grabbed a couple of beers and joined her on the couch. She surprised him by planting a big kiss on him. Her hand found his groin and rubbed. This was the on button for him – and for almost every other guy. Without warning, he grabbed her and forcefully threw her into the couch then pinned her down. It didn't hurt her, but she had lost control, quickly. His hands rode her shirt up and pulled down her panties. He rolled her over onto her stomach and spread her legs. With his hands he spread her cheeks, went south soon and she realized that she was being rimmed. This didn't really give her any real pleasure, but she didn't really mind the odd sensation because he seemed to be really enjoying licking her butt. That was until he slid a wet finger into her anus. It felt just too weird for her.

"No," she said. "Stop."

He stopped and was puzzled. "What?"

"Nothing up there. It is an out door only."

"Are you sure?"

"Yes. I don't do anal, so stop."

He agreed and went back to admiring her ass. He licked it and then he took off his clothes so he could rub his penis all over her ass. He moaned as he did it.

"Put a condom on," she said.

He whined about it, but put one on anyways. As he did, she turned onto her side to check him out. His penis was small, but his body was nice. He must work out regularly, she thought. Not as nice as ego boy, but easy on the eyes.

"Like what you see?" He asked.

"Yes. How often do you go to the gym?"

"Three times a week."

He shoved her back on her stomach. "Jesus, you have a nice ass."

"Ah, thanks."

"How often do you work out?"

She felt a sharp pain in her ass and screamed, "Get

that fucking thing out of there!" Even though he was only part way in it was a good thing that he wasn't that big.

He protested by saying, "Come on baby give it a minute, you will like it."

"No! Stop right now or I will call rape!" She managed to turn enough to be able to slap him across the face. This shocked him.

He stopped and got up. "Sorry," he said. "I don't know why I did that."

"Don't do it again or I will leave!"

"Okay."

"No anal!"

"Okay I get the message." He switched gears and entered her. "You don't know what you're missing."

"Fine, let me go home and get my dildo and fuck you up the ass."

"Really?" He sounded interested.

"What are you queer?"

"No! Why would you say such a thing?" He looked offended and confused. "Of course, I am not gay. I'm Greek."

This was getting too weird. All she wanted to do was to have a nice normal have sex. "Then prove it. Just screw me normal like."

"Okay."

"Better yet. Let me show you." She pushed him back and lowered herself onto his penis. She started riding and he grabbed her ass cheeks. Now that she was in control again, she was starting to enjoy it.

However, before she got too comfortable in being the boss, he decided to switch positions and she was on her back before she knew it. He started to pump her. He grabbed her arms and held them above her head, preventing her from moving. He increased his grinding. All that she could do was to stop wasting her energy by surrendering. He was in charge and have sexing her hard. She couldn't move and was forced to receive his penis. To her surprise, she liked this.

"Do you like that?"

"Oh, faster. Yes, god I love it."

This guy likes control, she thought, the little Greek that could.

She giggled at her own little joke. Then he stopped and pulled out.

"Down on all fours," he said.

"Promise no anal."

"Promise."

He slid it into her vagina and grabbed her waist as he admired her ass and the small of her back. The view was a little too much for him and he soon came, riding hard all the way. "Ahhhh!" He groaned. He fell off to her right side and laid down.

"That was great", he said. "You've got a great ass."

I've heard that before, she thought. "Ah thanks."

He pulled a blanket over himself and closed his eyes. "Goodnight," he said.

She rolled her eyes and got up. He didn't move and either pretended to asleep or actually was. However, after she freshen up in the bathroom and came back, he said, "If you want to, you can leave your number. There is a notepad by the phone."

I guess that I'm leaving, she thought.

She got dressed and left without saying anything more. She took the pad and wrote down "Kelly" and put the number nineteen beside it. "That's my number", she muttered. "There is no way that I'm seeing you again, you arrogant buggar." She gave him the finger, but knew that he probably couldn't see it even if his eyes were open.

"Goodbye," she said loud enough so he could hear it.

She opened the door, but before she left he came out of the bedroom wearing a housecoat. "You know that you don't have to leave," he said. His tone was a lot nicer than earlier.

"Oh, I know."

"Did you write down your number?"

"Yes, I wrote down my number," she said. A smile came to her face. "Goodnight." She closed the door behind her and tried to suppress a laugh. She wished that she had a web cam in his apartment to capture the look on his face when he reads: Kelly 19.

Fortunately, the elevator came quickly, signaling that she had made her escape successfully. What wasn't successful was her plan to be in control, but she didn't mind. It felt good.

That was different, she thought. Except for the anal, it was quite enjoyable. It was exciting to be dominated like that.

She wondered if she had threatened his masculinity and had inspired him to be rougher than normal. For research purposes she momentarily regretted not leaving her number. Then she thought better of it, he being a bit of an ass and all that. Maybe that was normal for him. Ugh!

She concluded that she must do more research to see if the guys would react the same to her aggressiveness. As she walked through the lobby, she contemplated doing some research right now, but she went home instead. This was definitely a new chapter in her Dicksinary.

OUT OF CONTROL

Kelly felt very depressed. In the mood she was in, everything was sad. Even taking a walk during her lunch hour didn't help. Just seeing a poster for a lost dog or cat sent her to the bottom and she saw one of each today. See reminded herself that the animal most likely wasn't dead, a number of things could have happened, including the animal returning and the owner forgetting to take down the poster. Still, she felt sad for the animals and the owner whom she has never met. And of course, she assumed the worst for all.

On days like this, all the cases were particularly hard to deal with. They were not fun to deal with on the bests of days.

So much unhappiness, she mused, all those people wronging each other.

She was almost crying as she peered at her computer screen. A knock on the door was a welcomed distraction from her client list.

"You okay girl?" Debbie asked. "You look like you're ready for waterworks."

She sighed. "I'm fine. It's these people who have screwed up their lives."

Debbie nodded. "Don't let it get to you. Do what you can for them and nail the deadbeat fathers."

"Yes, but is it all their fault? Some women drive men away. Like…" she scrolled down the screen, "this one…she is a total bitch. No wonder the guy bolted."

Debbie closed the door and took a seat at the desk. "It isn't our job to judge these people and it isn't like you to do so. What is wrong?"

"Nothing that I want to talk about."

Debbie peered at her. "Okay, new subject. "What are you doing tonight," she asked, "seeing Doug?"

"No, he's gone, remember?"

"I know, but he has made it a habit of reappearing."

"That's true, but not this time. We talked and decided that we weren't compatible. Well…I decided and I guess that he got tired of angering with me."

"That's too bad."

"Better now than later when we're tied down to each other."

"So what are you doing tonight?"

"I'm going to get really drunk and get laid."

She grinned and said wryly, "By anyone I know?"

"No."

"So who is he?"

"I don't know. I haven't met him yet."

Debbie was shocked and exclaimed, "Kelly!"

Kelly giggled weakly.

Debbie squinted her eyes. "Very funny."

She thinks that I'm joking, Kelly thought, but that's exactly what I'm going to do. I want to lose my self in lust and alcohol. It has to be better than this. She waved her hand at the screen. With that the quest for a L.I.T. was postponed indefinitely.

The rest of the day dragged on, but she got through it without losing it. It was a struggle and by the time that she fought the traffic and walked through her door, she was ready to bust it loose. First thing that she did was to get herself a beer and turned on the stereo. Going right for the hard stuff, she put on Back In Black.

I'm a rock and roll party chick who is into one-night stands, she thought. Okay, who wants to party with me?

She lost the office clothes and slid into her jeans, the ones that were a little too tight and left nothing to the imagination. Occasionally, she heard the phrase `camel toes' while wearing them. She lost the bra, rubbed her nipples and looked for the right blouse to put on. She caught her reflection in the mirror.

Hmmm, maybe I should just go like this, she thought. After all, it is perfectly legal for a woman to go topless in this state now.

She laughed because she knew that she would never do that.

She decided on a pink blouse that made her look cutesy, figuring that it would be a good contrast to the rough and ready mood that she was in. Dinner was heated leftover lasagna washed down with two more beers.

It was 7:30 by the time that she left her apartment. It was a nice night and everyone seemed to be out and about enjoying the weather. The Pussy Pub's patio was almost full and she got one of the last tables. She loved sitting on a patio on a warm summer's night.

The waitress took her order and as she was walking back in, that guy that she had seen everywhere was walking out.

He must have been talking with Matt, she thought. Seeing his boyfriend.

She watched him leave and wasn't shy about studying the way he walked. He was almost past her when he noticed her smiling at him. It took him a few paces to stop and retreat

"Excuse me," he said. "Can I ask you a question?

"Sure," she said, "have a seat and tell me your name." Her eyes had already undressed him.

He shrugged his shoulders and obeyed. "Sure, why not." He had a seat then added, "Daniel.

"Hi Daniel. I'm Kelly."

"Hi."

"Now, you're a `friend' of Matt's, right?"

He ignored her implications. "Ah yeah, we're buddies."

"I've seen you and him talking a few times. Each time it looked like a deeper conversation than most bartender/customer talks."

"That's what I was going to ask you, I've been seeing you everywhere lately."

She giggled. "I know. Here, at work, heck even on the subway."

"The subway, when?"

"Tuesday at Union Station. I don't think that you saw me."

He laughed. "And I saw you on Wednesday and I don't think you saw me. I was going to approach you, but you move pretty quickly in heels."

"You have to be pretty fast to catch me."

"That's what I heard," he said too quickly then wished that he could take it back. "I mean…"

She squinted her eyes and said, "So you have been talking to Matt about me then?"

He was caught and he knew it. "Yes, sorry."

"Sorry about what? Being interested. You are interested, right?"

"Oh yeah. You're a very interesting woman."

"Oh you think so, eh? What do you know about me?"

"Um…"

"Don't waffle. Talk."

"Well, according to Matt, you like to drink Bud."

Right on cue, the waitress approached and placed a bottle and a glass in front of her. Then asked Daniel, "and what will you have?"

"Same thing," he said.

The waitress left and Kelly said, "Well, right on the beer. Check."

"You live in the neighborhood."

"Check. I live a few blocks over."

"You're single."

"Check."

"You work for in family services."

"Check."

"You're very good looking."

"Oh, thank you." She snickered. "Check."

"You're pretty comfortable with yourself. Confident."

"Check."

"And you have a high sex drive."

"Double check."

He leaned over to whisper, "And you never seem to be satisfied. You go from man to man and only want more. Your thirst is consuming and it kills any chance of a monogamist relationship."

She peered into his eyes. "Why do you think that? We've only just met." Her tone was a little defensive.

"Because I'm the same way."

She relaxed. "You go from man to man?" She quipped.

"No…woman…you know what I mean. For people like us, one lover isn't enough."

"You are certainly very forward."

He sat back. "Sorry, I'm just talking. I can get a little intense and carried away."

No shit, Kelly thought. She looked away during the silence awkward. She started to check out men walking down the street.

The waitress brought his drink then left. She was quick tonight, Kelly thought. Matt must have had them ready.

With a lighter tone he asked, "So how was your day? Have a good one?"

"It was okay."

"Busy?"

"Yes."

"Listen," he said. "I didn't mean to insult you or to make you uncomfortable or anything. I'm sorry if I did."

"Okay," she said.

They sat in awkward silence for a few minutes.

"How long have you know Matt?" She said.

"Five or six years."

She leaned forward and whispered. "It that how long you two have been lovers?" Her tone was sharp and it was his turn to be on the defensive.

He squinted his eyes at her and didn't know what to say.

"I too can observe things." She said matter-of-fact. She squinted her eyes then giggled.

He coughed. "Touché. Does it bother you if we are?"

"No, but if you are, why are you talking to me?"

He smiled. "Because I prefer woman."

"Oh, is that the tension between you and Matt?"

"Tension? What tension?"

"Okay, the way that you too were talking I thought that you were fighting."

"Oh no, on the contrary, all is fine with us. We don't get together too often and haven't for a while. He's been seeing some guy."

"And have you been seeing someone?"

"Nobody special."

"Do you tell them about you and Matt? I bet that it causes problems."

"Yeah, it does. Most people can't handle…switch hitters. In their eyes, you must be one way or the other."

She laughed. "That's true." She was too drunk to care about his partying with men. She was just glad that she had a shot with him. She was wet and it sounded like this guy was always hard. Prefect.

"So, how do you feel about bisexually?"

"I have no problem with it." Actually she did when she thought about it, but right now she wasn't thinking. She was drinking. Also, she was probably drunk enough that she wouldn't remember most of this conversation.

"So you're not disgusted by it?"

"No, why should I. It is just sex."

He was pleased by that response.

"I've never met a guy who has admitted to being with another guy before. Interesting."

"A lot of guys do on the side. Guys just don't admit it. Women are more open with it."

"Some women are."

"How about you?"

"I need another beer."

"Can I buy you one?"

She flashed her bedroom eyes at him. "Just one?"

He melted. "Oh, you're smoking. I'll buy you as many as you want baby."

"Well, I've had a really lousy day and I want to get hammered."

"And nailed?"

She laughed. "Yes, I want to get hammered and nailed." She smiled at him in way that told him that he had the nailing job if he wanted it, but that was only stating the obvious.

"You're a very sensuous woman Kelly."

"Thank you."

He got the waitress' attention and ordered another round.

"So can I ask you a question?" he asked.

"Yes."

"Have you ever been with a woman?"

"I just answered it. Yes I have. Not too many, but a few."

"Do you like it?"

"Sometimes."

"Excellent." He sounded pleased.

"Okay my turn to ask a question. So what else have you done that is out of the ordinary, besides being a switch hitter?"

"That's about it.

"Threesomes? Foursomes?"

"A few threesomes."

"Men and female."

"A male/female couple and a same sex couple."

"Hmmm, busy boy."

"Oversexed boy." He said matter-of-fact.

"Nothing wrong with that. Until a few days ago, I was seeing a guy that was a monk in comparison.

He didn't really have a sex drive."

"Why did you even bother going out with him then?"

"Well, he looked and acted like a guy who had it all – and for some women – he does. He had a good job, was good looking, smart and funny."

"And a limp dick."

She was taken aback by his comment. "Yes. How did you know?"

"I tell you we are of the same mind when it comes to sex. God I hate people who aren't into it. There is nothing worse than a woman who just lies there and stares at the ceiling. Some women think that they're so beautiful that they don't

have to do anything else. Wrong. That might work on some guys, but not me."

The beers came and the empty bottles went back as they talked about their upbringings, families and generally got to know each other. Kelly lost track of how many she had and was shocked to learn that it was 10:30.

"So, how about another round?"

"No," she said. "Time to take me home. Bed me."

"That's sounds good."

He paid the bill while she went to the washroom. On her way back, Matt saw her. "I didn't know you were even here," he said.

"Just leaving. I was on the patio with Daniel."

"Oh," he said shocked. "That's good." He smiled. "He's a good guy. Have a great night."

Daniel and her walked down the street and as they turned the corner he pleasantly surprised her. She was talking about her family when he slipped his hand into her hand. She liked that. Romantically, he stopped and kissed her.

Very nice, she thought.

Inside, her apartment, she led him directly to the bedroom. For hours now, there was no doubt what was going to happen. In fact, at one point she had even told him that he was sleeping over tonight.

"Well, my condoms or yours?" He asked wryly.

"Mine until we run out."

"Okay then. Let's get busy." She was naked and on the bed before he had his shirt off. Impatiently she spread her legs and fingered herself. "Hurry up sweetie."

He dropped his pants and she admired the bulge

in his underwear. He dropped to his knees, drew her close and started to eat her. This was unusual. For her most men in her life just want to stick it into a.s.a.p. She moaned her approval loudly. Very loudly. She had been soaking wet for hours now and his tongue felt so good on her clitoris. With his hands he spread her lips and gave a long slow lick from the entrance all the way up to her clitoris. Her sounds of delight inspired him to do it again. He did then flickered her clitoris with his tongue while massaging her opening with his fingertip, a double play. He continued to torture her this way until she came.

She was so lost in pleasure that she didn't even notice him taking off his underwear and sliding on a condom. Before she knew it, he was sliding into her at a good pace.

"Oh okay, that's good." She said then realized something. "Condom! Stop! Put one on!"

He laughed. "Yes, already have." he said. He pulled mostly out to show her the condom.

She sat up to look at the thing half sticking into her. Good size, she thought. "Okay, good. You may continue."

Very slowly, he re-entered. For a while he went torturously slow and only increased the pace by small increments.

It was driving her crazy. "Faster."

"No."

"Why?"

"That's for doubting me."

"Very funny. Now get to work."

Slowly he picked up the pace and she moved to meet each thrust. She placed her hands on his ass and tried to get him to go faster. He resisted and continued with his original plan. She had other plans. To his surprise, she started to grind him from the bottom.

"Oh god," he said. "That's something new." The way she moved told him that this was one woman who loved the sex act.

"On your back," she commanded.

He rolled over. She squatted over him and took him in. None of this slow motion crap for her, she rode hard in the saddle, letting her hips rock, pivoting on his penis, engulfing it hen letting it go. With each hard thrust she squeezed around his penis as she violently tried to absorb as much pleasure from it as possible. It was his turn to arch his back. He came, but she didn't stop until she did as well. When finished, she landed on the bed beside him.

After a few minutes, he spoke. "You got me by surprise."

"I know."

"I liked it. Very exciting. I'm not used to such aggression from a woman."

"Next time, you can surprise me."

"Deal."

She wondered when the next time would be. She knew that she wanted there to be a next time. For the first time in a long time she hoped that this wasn't a one-nighter.

"Well Kelly," he said strongly. "Surprise, the next time is now."

"What?" She looked down and he was peeling the used condom off his fully

erect penis. It was pointing directly at her. He gave it a couple of strokes before putting on a fresh condom. "Spread them," he said.

She was shocked and had frozen. He grabbed her and was inside her before she knew it. "Ah...yes... um...oh god, fuck me," she said.

He rode her hard in the missionary position before he told her that he wanted to switch to the doggy position. He pulled out. Without saying a word she was down on all fours and waited for him. He placed his hands on her slim waist and enjoyed the view.

"You have a great ass," he said.

"Thanks, but more have sexing less talking."

He laughed and rammed it in. "Jesus," she cried. She loved his forcefulness and moistens around his penis. She was good. She felt sexy. He ass was in the air and not only was she being rammed but his hands were admiring it. "Do you feel how stiff I am?"

"Yes."

"It's because of the amazing view I have."

Never in her life did she feel as sexy as she did now! She didn't think that it was possible, but this fact turned her on even more. So much so that the excitement was all too much for her. A couple of good hard thrusts later she had the big O.

It was almost four in the morning, but neither one of them were sleeping. "You tired?"

"No, not really. What do you want to do to me?" There was surrender in her voice. Without a word she peeled off the blankets and spread her legs; an invitation that he quickly took her up on.

Kelly closed her eyes and concentrated on the sensation of receiving each thrust of his hard penis as it seemed to massage every nerve ending in her vagina. To say it felt good would be an understatement. She basked in total pleasure, trying to soak-up every once of it; trying to get more, wanting more, even though she knew anymore would be too much for her to handle. His rhythm increased and it pushed her closer to the edge.

The thought that she rarely even came this way was violently pushed aside by a wave of pleasure. `Jesus fucking Christ!!' She whimpered as she clutched onto his back, her nails digging into his hard muscles, her face pressed against his hairy chest. Affectionately she rubbed her face against his chest, even licking it a few times. She couldn't believe it when he increased his rhythm. It was faster and more forceful than before. It was intense; too intense for her to continue. She tired to resist, but something was building inside of her. Dozens of pants later, she surrendered to the wave of pleasure overtaking her body.

Watching her get off in the intense manner in which she did was too much for Daniel. With great relief he finally stopped trying to hold back allowed himself to cum.

She sort of dozed off, but was soon awake again. She couldn't help but to think of all the great sex. She was too excited to sleep so she watched him sleep. After awhile, she pulled back the covers, and took the soft penis into her mouth. Moisture from her mouth soon covered it and washed away the dried cum as it slowly came to life. He groaned in his sleep and became hard. She ran her tongue all over his shaft. Like an expensive car, she loved the way it responded to her slightest touch. He was barely awake yet he was hard as a rock. She deep throated him over and over again. When she though he was close she stopped. Well lubricated with her salvia she jerked him hard until he came. The salty liquid landed on her hand. She wiped it off then laid down to go to sleep.

After she had drifted off to sleep, the next thing she knew was that something was between her legs softly licking her pussy. She briefly wondered how he got into position without her waking up, but then forgot about questioning it, as she got lost in his tongue action, especially when his tongue concentrated on her clitoris and a finger circled her opening. She resisted coming for as long as possible but it felt too good that she was struggling with it. She came, they had sex again and they both feel asleep.

"Does that feel good baby?" Kelly asked. It was now about 5:30 am and they were at it again.

His eyes were clenched tight and he was grunting as he was pounding away. It pleased her how much he was enjoying her body. She felt desires. She too was enjoying the sensation of his penis sliding in and out of her. He picked up the pace and started to jerk. His nice steady rhythm was replaced with erratic hard thrusting movements. Kelly was pinned to the bed and it was all she could do but to take it. She knew that he couldn't last long, but she didn't mind, she loved this

He groaned as he came and after a good dozen thrusts he started to slow down. She giggled. "Wow sweetie that was intense." He opened his eyes and he was almost at a stop now. "You're pretty hot."

"Thank you." She kissed him then before she could

lean back he grabbed her and planted a big kiss on her lips. He started to slowly slide in and out of her.

"What are you doing?"

"Nothing."

"Are you hard again?"

"Yep, can't you feel it?"

"God, you're never satisfied," she said.

"Neither are you, so shut up." He laughed.

She giggled. "That's true."

He started pumping.

"Wait."

"What?"

"I want a new position."

"Which one? Haven't we done them all tonight."

"I've got one. Get up."

She retrieved a chair from the kitchen and told him to sit on it. With her legs on either side of him and the chair she lowered herself onto his penis. It slowly filled her pussy. By using her legs she was able to bob up and down on his shaft with speed. With her head thrown back, her hands on his shoulders she washed his penis with the wetness that was building inside of her. His penis was soaked and fully erect as it was being squeezed on every side at once. She let out a moan of pure pleasure. He opened his eyes to watch her svelte figure bounce up and down. She's an animal, he thought; so passionate, so horny.

He let out a groan as he felt the pleasure of cum flowing through his penis and out of his body.

At breakfast – which was around two in the afternoon by the time that they got out of bed, Daniel said, "Kelly."

"Yep."

"Me thinks that we're pretty damn compatible."

"Yep."

"I want to see you again."

"You leaving?"

"I was…"

"Ah listen guy, you're not leaving. You're staying. You still have some work to do."

He smiled.

"Hard labor?"

She laughed. "Yes."

UPGRADE 2.0

Not only was Kelly on time for work Monday morning, but for a change she didn't look like she was dragging herself in. Also, she felt as good as she looked.

"What happened to you this weekend?" Sara asked her. "I called a few times. Were you at Doug's?" Then she corrected herself. "No wait, he's toast."

Kelly grinned and shook her head.

"Were you at some guy's that I don't know about place?"

Still grinning she shook her head.

"Were you...oh, I give up. Tell me."

"At lunch. There's too much to tell you."

"Oh my god girl. You're downright giddy."

"It was a great weekend!"

On her way home, Kelly kept a lookout for Daniel without trying to appear that she was looking for him. `Bumping' into him would be nice, she thought.

She was a little disappointed that she didn't, but she knew that he would see him again soon. I had better, she thought.

While cooking dinner she couldn't stop thinking of him, wondering what he was doing and when they would get together again. Tonight would be too soon, tomorrow would be…oh, no, she thought. What bad timing. I finally met someone that excites me and my period is coming. Ugh! Well, anyway I hope that it comes tomorrow.

After dinner, she listened to her messages and returned calls when needed. Her mother and brother were first. Sara didn't need calling back; she had been briefed at lunch today. There were a couple of hang-ups, but she knew that they were only guys who sitting by their phones with a hard on. She understood their reasoning. Why bother to leave a message when she isn't at the ready.

All evening, she wondered why she felt a little lonely. She knew that Daniel wouldn't phone tonight; it wouldn't be good dating edict if he did, and still she wished that he would. Someone once told her or she read it somewhere that loneliness is not being with the person who you want to be with. And she wanted to be with him! She went to bed early and read for a while before turning off the light. She fell asleep hugging a pillow.

Like she knew he would, he phoned Tuesday night. However, instead of asking her to dinner, a movie or for a drink, he did something that surprised her.

He asked her to meet him for coffee on Wednesday.

At eight o'clock he was waiting outside of Starbucks. She pulled in and starred at him before she got out. Golf shirt, Cargos and nice shoes, he certainly dresses well, she thought. Nicely groomed. Short hair looks good on him. I'm glad that he doesn't have any facial hair. Not the best looking guy in the world, but not bad at all. Not bad at all!

Nervously, she checked her own appearance in the mirror before going out. She knew from experience that sometimes the passion between two people on their first encounter never repeated itself. She hoped that this wasn't the case with Daniel.

"You look great," he said. "It is good to see you again."

With his arm tenderly around her, he kissed her. He held the door open for her and Kelly noted that he was doing or at least trying to do everything right. Even though they just had an entire weekend of hot sex, he treated her like a lady. This pleased her.

She watched him from a seat as he got their orders. He seemed like he is a sensitive nice guy. How can I not fall for this guy, she thought. Then her natural suspicion kicked in. So what is wrong with him? Why is he still single at twenty-seven?

Her fault detector was in overdrive as she scanned for hidden problems. Stop it, she yelled at herself. Don't go looking for problems.

"Here you are," he said, placing her coffee on the table. He sat down and she looked away. "So, how has your week been so far?"

"Busy."

"Any interesting cases?"

"No."

"Really. I thought that you would come across some very interesting people."

"No, not really."

"Well on the weekend you mentioned how much you like your job, so there must be some interesting situations."

"Yes, but nothing that I should really talk about." Oh god, loosen up girl, she thought. You're making it difficult for this guy. She took a deep breath. "So how was your week?" She said as pleasantly as she could. "So far."

"Fine. We got a couple of jobs out, made some money so the bills will be paid."

"So you like being an architect?"

"Yes, to a point. It is a constant battle not to work too much. I put in a few

extra hours on Monday and Tuesday, but made sure that I left on time today. Too many people I know work their lives away making lots of money that they have no time to spend it."

"So how many hours do you work on average?"

"I make sure that I don't put more than five hours overtime per week. That way I can do a little extra and please the bosses without sacrificing my life."

"Yes we have a few people in our office that never leave. It seems the more work you do, the more that the bosses give you."

"Yes, it's our North American society. It's based on greed. Make money. More. More. More. Too much is never enough."

"Sounds like you're sick of it."

"A little. The pressure to work overtime is almost unbearable at times. I was asked again tonight. I can see why some people get caught in a trap. It is easier to give into the pressure than fight against the current."

"Which sounds like the voice of experience."

"Yes, I got trapped for the first few years. Now, I'm trying to break free. I just need a good reason to." He brushed his hand against her hand.

"Well, I won't let you work too much. Well, out of bed that is." She squinted.

"Uh. There are those eyes. The ones that drive me crazy."

"Easy big guy. We're talking right now. Slow down."

He smiled. "Okay, will do. Next subject. So when was your last vacation? And where?"

"Florida a few months ago. But the most fun was L.A."

"With who and why?"

"A girlfriend. Sara. Shortly before she got married. Maybe that is why it was so fun, because we were both free, no restrictions."

He nodded like he was processing the information. "Who did you go to

Florida with?"

"A different friend. It was fun, but it wasn't as fun."

"Female?"

"Yes. How about you? When was your last vacation?"

"I went to Cape Breton last summer."

"With who?"

"A girlfriend."

A momentary air of tension was cast between them before she said: "I guess

that we should talk about our history."

"Yes we should, I guess."

"Who first?"

"You."

She shook her head then asked, "So how long did you see her for?"

"A year."

"Why did you break up?"

He looked up comfortable and grunted. "Incompatible. And I worked too much."

"So what is your longest relationship?"

"That was it. I've never been able to find someone who is completely compatible."

He told her his dating history and the reasons why things never worked out. Even though he appeared to be completely honest, Kelly couldn't help that he was hiding something. She figured that she was just PMSing. Well, she hoped that it was only her. It was then when she realized what he meant by incompatible. He couldn't find someone who could keep up with him in bed. This fact eased her.

"So how long have you know Matt?"

Again, he looked uncomfortable. "Three years. Let's go for a walk. There are a few paths close to here. Perfect for strolling."

Outside, he asked, "So, I've done all the talking about me. Tell me about your history."

"Naw."

"Why not?" He took her hand.

"I'm boring."

"Listen, not only do I know that you're a little on the wild side, I like the fact that you are."

"Really?"

"You're a pretty exciting woman."

"No, not really."

She told him a little of where she grew up and of her family. She eased up and the eventually found a seat on a park bench. After a while of talking and laughing, he changed the light tone to a more serious one. He said, "I have a confession to make."

Uh-oh, here it comes, she thought. "Okay, good ahead."

"Normally, I ask the woman for dinner and that can be awkward sometimes. You can have great sex with someone one night and have nothing in common with them, so dinner can be very strange and disastrous. That is why I only asked you for coffee."

"Oh…" She didn't know what was coming next

"I hoped that it would be different with you and," he paused to smile, "I'm pleased that it is. I think that it has been great. I've really enjoyed talking to you."

"Yes, me too."

"So when can I take you out on a proper date? I think that you're something special."

"Really?"

"Yep."

"Why do you say that?"

"I just do that's all."

"There must be more than that."

He sighed. "Well…"

She peered at him. "Be honest. I'm a big girl. I can take it."

"Well, I know that you are a wild one and we've talked about that before. You've been with a lot of guys." He studied the guilty look on her face. "Remember Matt told me."

"Yeah, right. Okay. So that doesn't bother you?"

"No, I like that. It tells me that you like sex."

"Love it actually. I'm a little bit of a tramp." She groaned. "Oh, I shouldn't have said that."

"Why? I know already." He smiled. "I overheard you talking to your friends at Martin's last week. I found your attitude refreshing and the woman who I was with at the time, well…I found her attitude to be too typical of most women. They are too stuck up and most of them just lie there. So I find your high sex drive to be very exciting. Don't change."

"Well, if you don't mind that I've been with a lot of guys."

"Not a problem, my little wild one." She smiled. "Lets take a walk?"

"Sure."

As they started walking he brushed his hand against hers again. She snickered then he sheepishly grabbed her hand to hold it.

"Hmmm. Mr. Romantic."

"That's me."

Near the swings, he spun her around and grabbed her by the waist. Kissing was the natural next step. It got hot and heavy quickly, his hands exploring her assets. She pulled away and said, "I have something to tell you."

"What?"

"It is only temporary," He looked uncomfortable. "But my `friend' came a couple of days ago."

"Who is he? Or is it a she?"

She laughed and gave him a look. "Daniel."

The lights came on. "Oh, that friend."

"Yes."

He looked sad then joked, "That friend is no friend of mine."

"Well, it is better that this friend comes than not at all."

"Yeah, right. That wouldn't be good at all."

She looked around. "Come." She let him to a more secluded part of the park. It was dark enough so that nobody could see them. She leaned up and kissed him. "There is no reason why you must suffer too. Lean against the tree."

"Oh, I like your line of thinking." He obeyed and she unzipped his pants. While squatting she freed his penis from its painfully restricting place in his underwear. She stuck out her tongue and touched the tip of his penis and it responded by jumping. Circling her tongue around the tip, she teased it before slowly taking him into her month. With each of his thrusts she squeezed her mouth around his penis as tightly as she could, trying to create as much moist pressure as possible.

"God you're good," he said. "My little wild one."

After a couple of dozen good strokes she pulled by back to say, "Let me know when you're close to coming, okay?"

"I'm close now."

She took out a condom and put it over him. A dozen or so bobs later he filled the tip of it.

After he recovered, they continued their walk. "Thank you very much," he said. "That was awesome."

"You're welcome."

"You didn't have to do that."

"I know, but I wanted to. And besides what else do horny little sluts do." She

raised an eyebrow.

"Kelly. I didn't call you that. I didn't mean it like that."

"I know you didn't, but…"

He kissed her on the forehead. "You're not a slut."

"Yes, I am! You didn't call me that, but I am. I am a horny little slut who has to get drunk before she can pick up a strange guy to have sex. I'm sorry, but that is who I am. I'm not sure if I can change, even for you."

He smiled. "Who says that I want you to change?"

She was shocked. "What?"

"Listen, I want to take you out for dinner and a movie and…well, let's just say that I want to see you again and again. We'll take it one step at a time."

"Are you sure?"

"Very. Let me buy you dinner."

"That sounds good, but I've already eaten."

"Not tonight silly."

"I'm free Friday."

"I'll pick up at seven. Or should we meet right after work? I know a great little place near the station. What works for you?"

Kelly thought about the hassle of going home, getting ready and all that waiting. She decided to meet right after work. "But let's exchange work numbers because if I'm delayed, I wouldn't want to keep you waiting."

"Sounds good. When we get back to the cars."

Kelly didn't bother to pick up the phone Thursday night. Instead, she played the part of a hermit, taking care of the laundry, cleaning and making sure that she got her rest. The phone rang a few times; she recognized the numbers and decided not to pick up because she wasn't looking for a quickie right now. And besides, her thoughts were on

Daniel. She really liked him and he seemed to be totally taken by her. This was good, she thought. He is hiding something. And why is he so forgiving of my wild nights? Does he think that he can change me? Do I want to change? Can I change for him?

He is too perfect, she mused as she laid down on the bed and stared at the ceiling. A gentleman with a good job, dresses well and accepts me for who I am. Can I be so lucky?

She hoped so, but something told her that he was just being nice. Too nice.

Later on, she was excited and downright giddy; and of course, horny.

God what is wrong with me? She mused. All I want to do and all that I can think about is sex. Men, women, more men, and more women you name them, I want to have sex them. Dicks, breasts, and pussies you name it. I want to suck it. God I'm wet. I'm a sex-a-holic.

As she laid on her bed, undid her jeans and pulled them done, exposing her panties. Reaching into her panties she started fingering herself as a slide show of body parts flashed through her mind. She pulled off her panties and raised her blouse. She was getting into it now, very determined on getting off.

Rachel Richards

One finger in, one working the clitoris, oh Daniel's penis is so thick and pretty, she thought then licked her lips. I'm sucking it. It's filling my mouth and...

She came hard.

Relaxing in the afterglow, she came to the conclusion that she was a sex-a-holic and that she never wanted to change! Why should I? She thought. I am what I am and I never want to have sexing change.

She took off her jeans and panties and got out of the bed. Then she walked into the living room, taking off her blouse and bra along the way. She was totally naked by the time she got to the living room. She felt that being naked is very sexy.

Finding her favorite porn tape, she put in into the VCR and turned on the TV. She started touching herself even before she sat down. On screen some chesty blonde was getting royally screwed by a large penis as another blonde - half out of a maid's outfit - squatted over her face. The first blonde seemed to enjoy being in that position.

Doing and being done, Kelly thought, the perfect combination.

Kelly's moans matched the blonde's on the screen. Their sounds of pleasure were momentarily drowned out by the guy's grunting and words of prayer. "God, yes," he shouted. "Oh my god, yes!" Then he pulled out of the blonde's pretty hole and fired his load over her. When he was finished, the second blonde turned around and licked up the cum.

Now that's a good maid for you, Kelly joked. Will clean up any mess, anytime, anywhere.

Kelly squinted her eyes, quickened the pace and desired to clean her up. She pictured herself locked in a 69 with her. Both of her hands were clutching her tiny ass as she tried to shove her tongue as far possible up her pretty little hole. Just the thought of doing that was overwhelming to her.

"Ohhhh!" She came again.

After she recovered, she turned everything off and went to bed. Surprisingly, she thought of sex.

Don't I ever get enough?" She mused.

The answer was of course, no.

"I'm a sex addict," she mumbled. "I admit that freely," She chuckled. "And I love it. I never want to change. I want to have as much sex as possible with as many beautiful people as possible."

She stared at the ceiling and wondered, "Is that

who I am? Am I really an addict?

A quick scan over her sexual history answered that. Okay, she thought. I guess that I am. Now do I have a problem with that? She thought about it for a while then came to the conclusion that she didn't. Feeling peaceful that she finally admitted to herself who she was, she fell asleep quickly.

Dinner on Friday was great. Both the food and the conversation were of high quality. He surprised her when he told her that he had driven that day.

"Why did you do that?"

"Because I didn't want to have to take you home on the subway."

Getting a drive home was a nice touch. Getting the doors opened for her was even nicer.

"You're coming in, right?" She said.

"I would like to."

"I don't know where you can park."

"Well, can't I park on the street?"

"They ticket."

"How often?"

"Every second or third night I think."

"I'll take the chance."

Inside, she poured the wine and brought him a glass. Sitting beside him on the couch, she thanked him again for a great dinner.

"You're worth it."

"I'm not." She looked at him in such a way that made him wonder what was on her mind. He asked her. "You have a very expressive face Kelly. There is something on your mind. What is it?"

"Why are you single? You're an amazing guy. You're a gentleman, good looking, successful... what is your secret? Why did the other girls let you go?"

"Because I'm not perfect."

"Why did you and Diane break up?"

He took a sip of wine. "Well, I have a confession to make."

"Go on."

"I have a very high sex drive."

"That's not a problem nor is it a secret."

"It is for some girls."

"Oh and you fooled around on her and you got caught."

He looked repentive. "Yeah."

"She wasn't enough for you?"

"Once every three weeks isn't enough for anyone, never mind me and my high sex drive."

Kelly looked horrified. "Every three weeks! But what did she expect, if that all she wanted. Why were you with her?"

"Well, it was more at the beginning then it went all down hill from there. And after a while it was the only thing going down." He chuckled to himself.

"Did she actually catch you in the act?"

He smirked. "Oh yeah. She came over unexpectantly and heard us through the door."

"Oh wow." She tried to take it all in.

"I have a confession to make."

"Another one? Geez. What else can you tell me? That you're a Martian."

"Kelly!" He gave her a look.

"Okay, go ahead."

"Now promise me that you wouldn't get all

freaked out."

"Sure."

"Now, the reason why most of my relationships fall apart is..." He took another drink. She patiently waited. "...is that most woman can't handle some certain things."

"Like being fooled around on. I'm not too crazy about that either."

"Yeah, a...oh, shit." He sighed.

"Listen Daniel. I think that you're wonderful and I want to get closer to you. So what is it?"

"But I've told you already."

"You have?"

"Yes, the night we "met"."

"Really? God, I was so drunk and horny I can't remember what we talked about."

"Really?"

"Sorry."

"I don't know if I can tell you."

"Well apparently you told me before and we still got it on so it can't be that bad."

He looked at her. "That's true."

"Spit it out, boy."

"Okay...you asked for it. Ready?"

"Yes!"

"I like men. Diane caught be in bed with another guy."

"Oh." She was shocked and stunned.

"Sorry."

"Why? You're bi?"

"Yes."

"Right, I knew that already. Now I remember. I knew that you've been with Matt." She took a drink.

"Yes."

"Oh."

"Does it bother you?"

"That is who you are. You can't change."

"But some women can't handle it."

"Some women can't."

He cocked his head. "How about you?"

"Well, I've been with a few woman, so I'm bi too." She looked at him. "How can I look down on you for being with someone of your own sex when I've done it too."

He was almost giddy. "So you have no problem with it?"

"With the fact that you've been with guys in the past, no. I guess the problem is when you want to do it again. Do I want you cheating behind my back with another man? Ah, no! Nor do I want you to be with another woman behind my back."

"How about a threesome? Ever done one?"

"Oh yeah, of course. But with two girls and one guy, not two guys."

"Would you be interested?"

She thought about it. "In time, I think. Let me get to know you better."

"So you're at least open to the idea of it?"

"Oh yeah."

"Well that's good enough for me."

He smiled then took another drink. She echoed. After a few minutes, she asked, "So how did you and Matt meet?"

"In a gay bar. He was the one who I got caught

"Damn is he pretty. Is he as beautiful naked?"

He chuckled. "Want to find out?"

An image flashed through her mind that excited her. It was of Matt naked. The thought made her horny. "Daniel."

"Yes?"

"Do you mind doing if we stopped talking for a while?"

"No, not at all."

"Good. Screw me."

The next morning, he checked his car and was glad that he didn't get a ticket. He said that he to run a few errands, but he would pick her up around five for dinner. She was glad of the mini break. It gave her a time to recover and also to think of things. She was pleased how things were going. He was certainly the best thing that she has had in…years? Maybe ever, she mused. However, there was one thing that was questionable.

How do I feel about his `wildness'? She thought.

Can I handle it?

She had to admit that it was something new. Though she wasn't surprised by it. She did sense that he and Matt were lovers and she was right.

He is a total sex freak, she thought.

She was busy putting him down for it until she realized the contradiction. She came to the conclusion that it takes one to know one. So, with that thought she decided not to judge him for it and to concentrate just on the positive.

She was ready for him at five when he pulled up. His place was nicer than her apartment, but it didn't have the same warmth. "It needs a woman's touch," he said.

"That can be arranged." She looked around. "I have ideas."

"Like what?"

"Like moving," she said wryly. "Just kidding."

They chatted for a while as they had a few glasses of Shiraz. "So now that

you've had some time to think about it, what are you thoughts about what I told you."

"What, about you being a switch hitter?"

"Yeah."

"Well, it doesn't horrify me. I guess that I don't have a problem with it."

"Does it turn you on?"

"Yeah, a little I guess, but...I don't want you screwing anyone, a woman or a man behind my back."

"No fear of that. Promise."

"Good."

"So, do you think that I'm an oversexed pervert?"

"Yes, but it takes one to know one." She laughed.

"I'm glad that you don't have a problem with it."

She smiled weakly. "So what's the biggest dick that you've sucked?" She took a drink and watched his reaction.

"I've only been with Matt and a couple of others."

"Do you love him?"

"No! I don't love guys. Matt is someone who I just get together with from time to time."

"How often?"

"It depends if one of us is seeing someone. It could be as long as once every six months to a few times a month."

"Got any gay porn?" She asked.

"Ah, no."

"How much regular porn do you have?"

"Too much. You?"

"I have a few movies. Maybe a dozen or so."

"Hardcore?"

"Some hard, most of them soft."

"You're the first woman that I have met that actually has porn."

"I'm different."

"That's for sure."

"So are you, bi-boy." There was a little edge to her words and she was a little upset with herself that she had let it out. "Excuse me. I need to use the washroom."

"Sure."

Inside the washroom, she told herself not to sabotage this. When you go back, she told herself, change the conversation to something other than he being with guys.

He intercepted her on the way back from the bathroom and put his arms around her. It was clear what was on his mind and she didn't protest. She let him kiss her, nozzle her neck and undress her. However, she got an idea.

"Stop," she said.

"What?"

"Tonight, I'm in charge," she said playfully. "You will do what I say."

"Okay." He was grinning.

"Take your clothes off and get down on all fours. On the bed, of course."

He raised an eyebrow then obeyed. As she approached the bed, she said, "Spread your legs."

He protested. "I don't receive anal."

"Who said anything about anal?"

She got onto the bed and slid up between his knees. From there she was able to lick his balls and stroke his penis lightly with her fingertips. He moaned his approval. It became too much for him and he started to pull away. "Don't move," she commanded and smacked him on his ass for empathies, "until I tell you to." He obeyed and resettled his balls over her mouth.

"Gentle," he said.

"Did I give you permission to speak?"

He laughed. "Please suck my penis." He opened his legs to let her move up.

"Shhh!"

She repositioned herself so that she could take his penis in her mouth. One stroke, two strokes to cover it with salvia then let her tongue flicker just behind the head as her right hand stroke the base of the shaft. She pressed her tongue into that tender area then used her lower lip to get more pressure.

"Jesus fucking Christ!" He groaned. He was rock-ing so much that she had a difficult time hanging on. She had to grip him with both hands. This got him more excited and without warning, warm bitter fluid flew into her mouth. She waited until he was completely done before she swallowed. She couldn't remember the last time that she had done that. It was probably a number of boyfriends ago.

"God," he said. "I love women who swallow."

"Of course, you're a guy."

She awoke before he did. She wasn't used to sleep-ing anywhere else but her own place. Still, she didn't mind. It was refreshing and a bit of an adventure to find where the coffee was. It was on

the top cupboard above the coffee maker. Being a lot shorter that he is, she had to climb onto the counter in order to reach it. She couldn't find the filters, so she used a paper towel. It dawned on her that maybe he doesn't use filters.

Men are illogical, she thought as she studied how he had set up his kitchen. To her it looked he hadn't given any thought. She joked that he might keep the filters in the front hall closet.

While she was waiting for the coffee to brew, she walked into the living room to look around. As impressed as she was by how he was treating her, his place reminded her that he was still just a guy. He wasn't exactly a slob, he was better than most, but to her, the place could use a real good cleaning, something more than him running the vacuum over the carpet once a week.

She sat on the couch and stared out the window at the downtown core. Not a bad view, she thought.

She tried not to think of what she had learned last night. She found it both disgusting and a turn on at the same time. Two dicks touching each other, cumming in each other's mouths. Giving it to…

She pictured Matt down on all fours with Daniel behind him, ramming it home. This didn't turn her on, but picturing Matt naked did. Also, Daniel's body was burning in her mind as well. She shivered then touched herself to realize that she was wet. No need to masturbate when I have a perfectly good L.I.T. in the next room.

Gently, she climbed into the bed and pulled of the sheet. She pressed her lips to his soft penis, causing it to stir. The fact that it was covered with dry cum didn't stop her from licking it. When it rose to half erect, she took it in her mouth. He moaned in his sleep. It didn't take long for it to get erect enough to slip on a condom.

"Ready or not," she said as she lowered herself onto his erection, "here I come to swallow you whole."

He woke to the smell of freshly brewed coffee and a woman riding his erection.

"Welcome to paradise!"

She said, "Good morning," then picked up speed.

"Oh, my favorite way to wake up."

After breakfast, he asked if he could make an observation.

"I guess so," she said. He really is a very serious guy, she thought.

"You know you don't really dress the part. You're a sexually exciting woman, but you dress like a...a bit of a prude."

She looked hurt. "Okay point taken."

"What I'm trying to say is that I would like to buy you a few new outfits; outfits that are classy yet sexy. Want to go shopping?"

"Ah, yeah. But..."

"Don't worry, I can afford to buy you a few things. And besides, I want to."

She laughed. "I've never met a guy who volunteered to go shopping with me."

"But only for certain things. I will gladly go with you if you're going to try on something sexy."

"Hmmm...I'm starting to think that if it has to do with sex, then you're into it. You're a bit of a perv."

He smiled. "Takes one to know one fellow pervert."

"I have no problem going to bed with a man if I think that he is cute and he treats me well," Kelly said.

"How about when you are with a women?"

"Oh they're just so soft and pretty," she said licking her lips. "It is very tender, very beautiful. I like them too."

"So why not become a lesbian?"

"Because sometimes I love a good hard pounding. A nice hard penis filling my pussy. There is no better feeling."

"And women?"

"After my first sober experience with a woman, I fully understood why men love women so much. They're so soft and delicious, so fun to play with."

"What do you like the most about them?"

"They're soft and pretty."

"What is your favorite body part?"

"Breasts. I like big breasts. Maybe because I like what I don't have." She laughed. "You?"

"I like woman who like having sex for the pure enjoyment of it, not for money, power or revenge, but for the shear pleasure of it."

"Wow that's me. I love being invaded as long as I get to determine where and when I get invaded."

"I like passion. The passion in a woman's eyes when she really likes a guy and can't wait for him to do all the right things to get between her legs."

She flashed her bedroom eyes at him. "Daniel."

"Yes."

"Plough me like a field," she said then laughed. "Sorry. No laughing during sex."

ENLIGHTEN ME

Even though it was on her mind, she didn't tell Sara or anyone else about her concerns. This was a private thing for her to work out. She knew that she really liked this guy and it was clear that he was good for her. These days, she was getting to work on time and was well rested; maybe a little sore down there, but well rested and not hung over. She wasn't drinking as nearly as much as she used to and that was good. And the sex was plentiful and he had no problems with his equipment. It was working fine, maybe too fine and too often.

God he is horny bugger, she thought. He likes sex so much that he even sleeps with men sometimes.

She tried to accept it, but she had problems with his freeness. I think that I have met my counterpart, she thought. I don't know if that is what I want? Lots of sex, yes, but if he likes guys to then he has to go outside of the relationship to do that and that wouldn't be good.

Having him cheat with another guy was not only a strong possibility, but also something that she knew would probably happen. She knew she didn't want that. Thinking of it, was stressing her out. She finally decided that in time things would work out one way or the other.

Meanwhile no one knew of her internal turmoil. This was clear during lunch with the only person who could spot her dilemma.

"You don't have to say anything because we all can see that he is good for you," Sara told her. "When do I meet him?"

"Yes, he is," Debbie said. "We all can see the change in you, for the better."

"Yes, I feel good," Kelly said. Still, she was uncomfortable talking about it for a variety of reasons. For one, she didn't want to jinx it.

"It's about time that you settled down," Linda said. "God intended one man and one woman to be together for entirety. It is no wonder that you feel better. It is god's way and the quicker you stop fighting him and start living the way you're intended to live, the better you will feel."

Kelly looked away. Needless to say, she didn't need to be preached to. To her, it was a huge arrogant, "I told you so," from Miss Perfect housewife. For a fleeting second, Kelly seriously considered seducing Linda's husband. He's probably so sexually repressed that he wouldn't last a minute with me, she thought. But then again…

She remembered what he looked like and decided that it was a bad idea. The image of Linda and her fat husband doing anything was not a pretty picture.

Sara quickly changed the subject for her friend's sake. However, Kelly was in a mood to lock horns, so she brought the subject back to god and sex again by saying, "So what happens if a person is gay or bisexual, must they live with someone that they're not attracted to?"

"Oh, we pray for people like that all the time. We cast the demon of perversion right out of them."

Sara laughed and tried to lighten the mood, but Kelly won't have it. "So, if someone's view doesn't line up with yours, then they're demon possessed?"

"Yes, that is right. My view is the bible's view so that is the correct one. It isn't mine originally."

"Does it tell you what to have for lunch too? Does it tell you what to wear? How to wear your hair?"

"Yes, it does actually. In the book of…"

"And what to think, feel and have you ever had an orgasm in your life?"

"That is none of your business." It was Linda's turn

to be on the defensive.

"And my life is none of yours, so back the have sex off and never preach to me again!"

"Well…" Linda said. "I'm be praying for you."

"And I'll be fucking for you."

Kelly got up and left the table. She was steaming and the others were shocked. This wasn't like Kelly who hardly ever cared enough to get mad. Sara followed her and caught up with her on the street. "You okay?" She said. "Don't let that narrow minded preacher's wife get to you."

Kelly glared at her and kept walking. Sara found it hard to keep pace and told her to slow down a little.

"Is there something that you're not telling me?"

"No, I'm just really sick of people ramming their opinions in my face. Selfness is not wanting what you want for your life but is demanding that other people live the way that you want them to."

"By that definition, Linda is a very selfish people. But look at her, she isn't good looking and doesn't really have much going for her. She's probably very grateful if her fat husband gives it to her once a month."

Kelly stopped, looked at Sara then said wryly, "I think that she gets is every Saturday at 8:15, rain or shine. Wake up. Do husband. Do the laundry. Do..."

Sara grinned. "Yes, but only thirty to forty strokes. No more. No less."

Kelly laughed then sighed. "Sorry, but I just can't live the way that everyone seems to want me to live."

"No one is asking you to. Well...okay, Linda is, but who cares about her. She is a lost cause. Forget about her. Do what is best for you."

Kelly nodded. That was it, of course. She just needed to be reminded. "Now, what do I do about dealing with..."

"Just ignore her. You know that any confrontation she will only think that it is persecution."

When Kelly got back to the office, she buried herself in her work. It was the best way for her to ignore everyone without it being obvious. To her credit, Linda did come to her door to apologize that she had offended her. Kelly said that she was sorry for getting so angry and added, "I just can't live the way you do. I can't live my life by some book that was written thousands of years ago."

"Well, God's wisdom never goes out of date."

Kelly looked at her. "Let's agree to disagree on that. I think that we shouldn't talk about certain things."

Linda gave her a condescending look that Kelly interpreted as, "Guilt is too much for some people to handle." Fortunately, Lynda left without saying anything else.

On the subway ride home, she looked inward. She knew that she was and never would be a bible thumper, yet she didn't care if that what other people wanted. She accepted that in them. It just wasn't for her, that's all. Sex and drinking, that is what she liked. The drinking she was happy to keep mostly to the weekends and the sex, well...

Daniel is pretty damn good, she thought, the best that I've had since Bill. Not to say that Bill was better, just different. John is pretty good too, but he is married. Bye bye. Now, the million-dollar question is: is it worth it to be with someone who is as wild as I am?

She had a quiet evening at home and a thought hit her as she was getting ready for bed. I'm not really all that wild. And I guess that Daniel isn't as well. We're just a little freer than most people I know.

Kelly was bored. Not bored of Daniel, but just in need of something different, something exciting. To his credit, Daniel had kept her interest longer than anyone else had in years. The more that she thought about it, the more that she wanted him.

That old familiar feeling came again and she welcomed it, giving it the freedom to build. She wanted to be touched and the more she thought about who would be doing the touching the more she wanted to be groped, ravished and after a significant period of teasing and pleasing eventually rammed.

And she knew exactly who she wanted to do it to her. She picked up the phone and when he answered she said, "Hello – what's you doing?"

"Nothing much. What are you doing?"

"Getting wetter by the minute."

"Oh." He sounded shocked, but pleased. "Really?"

"I'm really to get laid a.s.a.p. How fast can you get here?"

"What are you wearing?"

"Cut-off shorts and a t-shirt. No bra."

"Nice. Are your nipples piercing through your t-shirt? If not touch them until they are."

She obeyed and she closed her eyes, enjoying the sensation.

"Now open your shorts and slid a hand down there. You know what to do."

"You want me to touch myself?"

"Yes I do."

She balanced the phone between her shoulder and cheek while her left hand played with her right nipple and the other hand slid into her panties and was rubbing her clitoris. For his benefit she emphasized her moans of pleasure. "I wish that you were here on top of me right now," she said between pants.

"Soon baby. Soon. First we're going to put out your little fire."

"It isn't little."

"It never is with you. I love that about you. You're a lady of passion."

"Take out your penis and stroke it for me."

"I already am. I've even lubed it."

"Really?"

"Yep."

"Let me hear it. Put the phone up to it and stroke it." He obeyed and she heard a sound of his hand jerking his moist penis. This made her wetter and she intensified her own efforts. Her left hand abandoned her nipple – which was protruding against her t-shirt – and slid it down to help her other hand satisfy her wet pussy. With one action she took off her shorts and panties.

"What are you doing?" He asked.

"I took off everything, but my t-shirt so I can touch myself easier."

The index finger on her left hand massaged the opening of her vagina as the other hand continued to flicker her clitoris, she was feeling pretty good and was pushed over the edge when he said, "Picture us on a beach in Cancun. There is no one around; the moonlight is dancing off the waves that are softly crashing against the beach where we're making love. My hard penis is slowly sliding in and out of you.

"Are you fully erect?" She said between pants.

"Yes, I'm always am when I'm with you."

"Oh god," she moaned slowly. She was at the edge. "I love your big thick penis! It is beautiful. I love looking at it, touching it, sucking it and feeling it inside me."

"And I love putting it in you. I would like to nail you in Mexico. Would you like that?"

"You can nail me anywhere that you want to. Just fill my pussy."

"That isn't hard to do. Your pussy is so tight and wet." With that thought he let out a groan.

"Come for me," she said. "And let me here it."

When he put the phone down close to his penis, she could hear his quick strokes and his groans in the background. He let out a loud groan when he came. She came right after.

Sleep came quickly to her and she was refreshed when she saw Daniel the following evening. With a clear head, she told them that they needed to talk.

"Okay, what's on your mind?"

"I'm not completely comfortable with something."

"And I know what. Hmmm…don't worry. I don't plan to sleep with anyone behind your back, male or female."

"So you'll do it right in front of me," she said wryly.

He blew her a kiss. "If that's what turns you on baby."

Her face fell. "Ah...um..."

"She that's it, isn't it? You don't like the fact that I go both ways even though you have done it."

"Well..."

"Talk about a double standard. Our society says that it's okay for woman to go

both ways, but frowns upon men doing the same thing."

She nodded. "You're right, it's a double standard."

"I'm sorry that you're having a problem with it, but I wanted you to know now and not down the road."

"I'm glad that you told me. You're right, it is better that I know now and not later."

"Are you okay?"

"Yes, I think."

"You know, it's not like I woke up and decided to do this. It kind of happened. Maybe I should tell you how it happened."

She sighed. "I'm listening."

"Really?"

"Yes. So what was your first experience?"

"It was in Mexico. A buddy and I went down to Cancun on vacation, like a million of others before. We were both twenty. Anyhow, the very first night that we're there, we met these two British broads and the next thing I know. I'm riding the brunette on my bed and I look over and I see the blonde naked on all fours with a huge penis slowly sliding in and out of her. Jim would pull it out almost all the way then fill her up to the max. The chick was in ecstasy. I knew that I shouldn't look but I couldn't stop staring at Jim's penis disappearing and reappearing. He saw me staring and said, "Get into doggie and do the same."

I obeyed and soon we were in sync. We watched each other as our dicks disappeared. Gradually we picked up the pace. Fuck did that turn me on! Needless to say, I filled the condom quickly. After-wards the girls decided to swap partners so they could do the same as they rode us.

Anyhow, the next day I couldn't get the image of his long thick penis out of my head. I yelled at myself. I'm not queer! I have sex with girls! I'm not queer!

While swimming I couldn't help to notice his body. All along I've always admired his body, but thought nothing of it. Now, I couldn't stop the image from flashing in my head. I was doing okay by replacing that image with one of the numerous babes walking around. That is until Lisa took up the chair beside us. She was a little older, curly blonde hair, very pretty and had a great rack. Of course, they weren't real.

It didn't take long for the conversation to get to the heart of the matter. She said, "I have a fantasy."

"What is it?"

"I would love to get nailed by two young studs at the same time."

The next thing I knew she is opening her hotel room to let us in. She poured us a few drinks and asked us about our experiences. She had told us some of hers and it was pretty damn hot. We both had very noticeable erections in our bathing suits, especially Jim.

She saw me looking at it. "Ever been with another guy?" She asked.

"No."

"Do you like it when two women get it on?"

"Yes, of course."

"Well, I like it when two men get it on."

"Really?"

"I love it." She gave a hot sultry look. "It gets me really wet."

"Well, I guess we could do a little," Jim said.

"What do you want us to do?" I asked

"Play with each other's dicks."

Jim slid off his bathing suit and I followed. Lisa voiced her approval at our erections and I couldn't help starting at Jim's huge penis. He sat on the edge of the bed and said, "Suck me."

I dropped to my knees leaned forward and kissed the head. It felt weird. Even though I've touched my own penis a number of times Jim's felt strange, almost rubber like. Then I took a little in my mouth, then a little more then before I knew it I was deep-throating him, and loving it. Jim was too.

Lisa came behind me and started to stroke me. "Give me a taste," she said.

Leaning over my shoulder she sucked the tip as I tongued his shaft. It didn't take long for Jim to cum and for Lisa and I to do it.

"I have to admit, that does sound pretty hot."

"It was."

"So was it a one time thing with him?"

"God no. For the rest of the vacation if we weren't screwing a chick we were sucking each other." He laughed. "I left so much sperm in Cancun."

"Oh my."

"Hey, I was young."

"So what is next? Now that you're not so young?"

"Depends. What do you want to see happen."

"Well…" She smiled then buried her face in her hands. "I'm such a bad girl."

He was laughing. "Go on."

"I've always had the hots for Matt…" She licked her lips.

"Me too." He felt movement.

"Do you think that he would mind me being with me?"

"He doesn't have a choice. I told him that from now on, if he wants me, you're part of the package."

"You've already talked to him about it?"

"Ah yeah. Well, he broke up with that guy. So he's between boyfriends right now. He phoned the other day wanting to come over to…well, cum."

"And did he?"

"No. I said that I wouldn't cheat on you behind your back."

"Just in front of me."

"Right."

"So is he interested?"

"You don't have a problem with seeing me with someone else?"

"Well, you've already been with him and if something serious between you two was going to happen, it would have happened a long time ago. You're just bed buddies, I know that. I will try it once and if I don't like it, I will say stop and it has to stop right then and there, agreed?"

"Agreed."

Daniel picked up the phone. Kelly asked him what he was doing. "Calling Matt," he said. "There is no time like the present."

"Really?"

"Hi Matt," he said into the phone. "How are you?"

"I'm good. I'm here with Kelly...yes things are going great...listen we were about to get naked and have fun and we wanted to know if you wanted to join us...yes, she's fine with it. Apparently, she's had the hots for you for some time...okay, see in a bit."

He hung up. "He says that he's got a hard one just thinking about it. You know...actually, you probably don't know this, but he does sleep with woman occasionally."

She opened her mouth, but nothing came out.

"Yes, he would have done you, but you never gave him a chance. You were always out the door with some average Joe before he knew it."

"Damn!"

Daniel answered the door and Kelly waited nervously on the couch. Matt

greeted Daniel with a kiss that lasted a little too long in Kelly's opinion. Now don't get jealous girl, she told herself. There is plenty of cock for everybody.

"Hi Kelly," Matt said as he came over. "How are you?"

She stood up and he gave her the same kiss that Daniel just got. Daniel approached them from the side and put his arm around both of them. He kissed the side of Kelly's face and repeated kissing her as he lowered down to her neck. Seeing this Matt broke off his kiss and echoed the kisses down Kelly's left side. By now, Daniel had a hand one each of their butts and Matt was grinding his crotch into her crotch.

"Oh god," Kelly moaned.

"So we should keep going?" Daniel asked.

"Hell yes. Take me!"

Matt slid down her body until he was in position to rub his face in her pussy. Kelly wished that her jeans weren't on and said something to that effect. Before she knew it the guys had them off her and Matt was licking her panties, which were now being soaked from both sides. Standing behind her, Daniel gently massaged her breasts and nibbled on her neck. Kelly was lost in the passion. Her brains were receiving reports of pleasure from various parts of her body at once.

"Should we stop?" Daniel teased. He raised her shirt over her head.

"No!"

The guys laughed.

Without warning, she was airborne and was being carried to the bedroom with only her panties on. She snuggled her head into Daniel's chest. She was doing very well right now. Very well. She loved the attention from two guys. She wondered why she never did this before.

Matt slid off her panties as Daniel gently laid her on the bed. Kelly spread her legs to let Matt go down on her. She stroked the top of his head with both hands and leaned back to enjoy his technique. She didn't know, but by this time Daniel had taken off his clothes and was in the process of taking Matt's pants off. Once free, his penis was stroked and sucked. For a few minutes, everyone was content.

"Daniel," she called. "Where's your penis? I want to get ridden and suck at the same time."

As Matt slid on a condom, Daniel stuck his penis in her face. "You want this?"

He asked.

She took it in her mouth and sucked. Without warning she was penetrated by Matt. She groaned as she sucked and screwed. Matt's rhythm was good for someone who normally receives. She was lost in the passion and didn't notice that since Matt's face was in proximity to Daniel's penis and that he was helping. She first noticed his presence when she started down the shaft as another tongue was coming up.

"Oh my," she said. "Fancy meeting you here."

"Didn't I tell you that I know all the best spots?" He kissed her, deeply and passionately. He also increased his rhythm. She threw her head back and Daniel pulled away. She was wondering where Daniel's penis had gone to until she saw him over Matt. Oh my, she thought. No wonder Matt's rhythm changed. He's getting it up the ass.

She wondered how she should feel about the fact that her boyfriend's penis was now sliding in and out of another man while she had another man's penis inside of her. Right now, she was a little jealous at seeing Daniel's eyes squint indicating that he was enjoying himself. She found it both disgusting and exciting.

Daniel opened his eyes and looked at her. "How are you babe?"

"Good. You know that I'm only happy when I have a nice big penis inside of me."

"You look great. I guess the question is how is Matt

doing?"

No answer from him, just grunts.

Kelly raised her head around Matt's and kissed Daniel. She stroked the hair back from his face. "Cum baby," she said. "Cum all over my breasts."

He increased his humping and after a dozen or so strokes, he pulled out, got the condom off, pushed Matt aside and sprayed Kelly's chest with cum. Both Kelly and Matt were impressed by the amount. Matt watched with interest.

"Apparently," he said to Kelly, "you're suppose to wait ten to fifteen seconds after cum has left the body for any AIDS poison to die." As Daniel went down on her, Matt counted to twenty then started to lick Daniel's cum off Kelly's breasts. Seeing this and feeling Daniel's overactive tongue pushed her over the edge. She came with intensity.

"So much for round one," Daniel said.

Round two involved all three of them stacked on top of each other. Kelly was on the bottom with Matt on top of her, have sexing her in the mission-ary position. Daniel was giving it to Matt up the ass. Kelly's only request was that they both didn't put their weight on her like last time. This was easily done as Matt used his strong arms to prop himself up; the only weight that Kelly was the thrust of his penis into her and she was free to squirm underneath him. Each stroke was strong and deliberate which Daniel matched.

"Don't cum yet," Kelly told Matt.

He like out a moan that indicated that this might not be a possibility. He was in ecstasy. Daniel and Kelly were having a pretty good time too.

"Nobody cum,' Daniel said. "Hang on for as long as possible."

Daniel increased his speed, which caused Matt to pump harder and faster and Kelly loving it. She watched as the two hunks were lost in lust and admired their bodies as the best she could from this angle.

"So pretty," she said. "So sexy. So…"

She was the first to cum and it set off a chain reaction.

HER OWN PATH

Both Kelly and Daniel did something that their work strong ethic hardly let them do. They both phoned in sick the next day so that they could continue to enjoy Matt. Also, they needed to catch up on the sleep that they didn't get that night. Besides the odd pang of jealousy and a few aches and pains Kelly liked the experience. So much so, that she agreed to do it again sometime soon.

It was Thursday night by the time that she got home. In the meantime, she realized that it was just sex and there was no sense getting jealous about seeing her boyfriend with someone else. She wondered if would apply if it was another woman? It shouldn't, she decided.

Well, if I'm going to embrace this free lifestyle I might as well go all the way, she thought.

She made a phone call. "Hello Steve," she said, "how are you?"

"Good. We called you a few weeks ago," he said, "you've been busy? Gail and I were hoping to get together with you."

"Ah, yes. Sorry that I didn't get back to you, but I've been seeing this guy."

"Oh," he sounded disappointed. Still, he asked, "How's that going?"

"Great! And I would like to see you and Gail soon."

His mood brightened. "Really? When?"

"Which leads me to ask you a question…"

"What?"

"My boyfriend would like to be part of it."

Silence.

"Steve? You still there?"

"Ah, yes. I don't know. I don't feel comfortable about being with another guy. I'm not a fag."

"It can be hands off for you two."

"I don't know if I want to see Gail get it from another guy. Sorry but, no."

Kelly bit her tongue. What a jerk, she thought. He can screw another woman, but she can't touch another guy. Double standard. Instead, she said, "Well, I'm in a relationship now, so if you want me then my boyfriend has to be there too. Think about it. Talk it over with Gail and get back to me if you're interested."

"Okay, I'll do that," he said. "And if you change your mind and when you break up with him we would love to party with you. Anytime."

"Ah geez thanks Steve." Her sarcasm was lost on him.

She felt the pang of regret after hanging up. Yes, she would love to get together with them, but that would mean cheating on Daniel, which wasn't worth it.

It didn't take long for her to find out something about Daniel, which she didn't like. Well, besides all the fag stuff that she still wasn't comfortable with and probably never will be, there were a couple of issues. One was that he was intense. Very intense. He seemed to have one speed only, fifth gear. And because of this he basically hijacked the relationship. She felt like she had lost any say and she felt trapped. Again. Only this time it wasn't about sex.

One night after dinner she automatically found herself getting ready to go out. Daniel was working or something; she couldn't remember what he said on her voice mail, mostly because she didn't really care. She needed a break from him. Without as much as a second thought she found herself in the

Pussy Pub. Her intentions were to go in to talk with Matt, but as soon as he got there she found out that he wasn't working tonight. She knew that she should have left but a song came on that almost made her cry. It was Queen's, "I Want To Break Free."

This made her sad because it was exactly what she wanted. Yes, she really liked Daniel, but she was a free spirit that wouldn't be controlled by him or by anyone. She decided that if he wanted her then he had to take her just as she was.

"How can I cheer you up?" A man asked her. He was tall and good-looking. Short hair and looked like he was in very good physical condition.

"Hi," she said smiling.

When they got back to her place, she started to put the moves on him, but he was reluctant to go further than kissing. And even that was pretty tame. Finally, she stopped and asked, "What is it?"

"I should inform you that I'm a police officer."

"Oh, okay." She continued stroking him. "What does that matter?"

"Listen I can't."

"Are you married?"

"No."

"What then?"

"I'm on the job."

She looked confused. "So? I've done a cop on the job before. In uniform even."

She smiled.

"No, that's not it. We thought that you were a pro. We've been keeping an eye on the Pub for a while now and you have been quite the regular. We'll you used to be."

She looked hurt. "So you don't want me? This was just part of your job?" She weld up.

"Yes, but…I don't think that you're a pro."

"No, I'm not a pro. I'm just a nymph."

She felt terrible about who she was and guilty for what she wanted to do. This was the worst of both worlds.

He noticed her weld up. "I'm sorry miss."

She was angry. "Take me or leave."

"If I wasn't on duty I would."

"Well, come back when you're off."

He smiled. "Maybe I will."

The next night Daniel was over and she was obviously moody. He asked her what was wrong.

"I'm incapable of having a normal relationship," she said.

"Who wants a relationship that is…" he used his fingers to form quotes when he said, "…normal?" He smiled. "I don't. Normal is boring."

"I don't know, Daniel."

"Don't worry about it, babe. Let's have fun."

"Before we go any further, there is something you should know," Kelly said. "I like you. I really do and I don't want to hurt you."

"What is it?"

"I am a nymph. There is no other way to put it. I love sex. I need lots of it. I've never met a guy that could keep up with me."

"Until now."

She looked at him. "I've messed around on you."

"Really? With who?"

"No, I haven't been with anyone else since we've been a couple but I've certainly thought about it."

"So you've wanted to mess around, but you haven't had the time to do so yet?"

"Yes, basically. It has nothing to do with you. It's me."

He snickered. "Oh that line sounds familiar. Usually it's the guy who uses it."

"No..." she said. "I'm not saying that I want to stop seeing you, it's just that I can't promise not to cheat on you."

"Oh I see."

"I'm sorry."

"How about if you cheat <u>with</u> me?"

She looked confused. "What do you mean?"

"Whenever you get the urge to wander let's go pick up some guy and have sex with him together."

"What happens if the guy that I want doesn't want to be naked with another man?"

"Then he can forget it."

"What happens if I want to have sex him anyways?"

He glared at her. "Well..."

"You know just a one time thing?"

"...as long as it's is not an ongoing thing...I

guess...if that is what you want, but I really don't like the idea. So...no, I don't want you cheating on me."

Remembering last night and the whole incident with the cop sadden her. She was at a crossroads. In one direction was her old lifestyle, which she loved and in the other was Daniel, whom she was trying to pull away from. However, deep down she knew that she didn't want to leave him. She wanted both.

Seeing her so upset, he tried everything to cheer her up, but it only pushed her away. Later, when he was gone she wondered why she had gotten so defensive with him so she called him. However, before he was able to pick up, she hung up and decided that the dishes needed to be done first. Doing them gave her time for her brain to organize her thoughts. They came together quickly. She told herself what the real problem was. She was very uncomfortable about all this fag stuff, knowing full well that it was a double standard. Girls can play with both girls and boys, but boys can't play with both. They have to pick one team. Society doesn't really mind the gay man, but it hates the bi male. The bi-female is more than accepted by society, she is loved.

She hated Daniel right now! She clearly wasn't happy. She was out of her comfort zone. She came to the conclusion that he is a fag but doesn't know it. She broke a glass and that sparked a temper tantrum. She threw a plate against the counter then another before running to the bed crying. She was clearly not happy she was out of her comfort zone.

Truth of the matter, he scared her. He was something special and she wasn't used to that. He didn't fit her profile of men. He was different. Better. However, she didn't see it.

She once wrote in her Dicksinary: "For me the best way to clear my head of problems is sex. It takes my mind off things. I guess it gets me off in more ways than one."

When the tears started to fade, she came up with a plan. She was going to use her old way of solving this problem. The more that she thought about it, the more excited she got.

As activate as she has been sexually, a lot of men have her phone number and vice versa so it wasn't difficult for her to arrange a special party. Within a couple of hours, the fourth and last guest showed up. By then Kelly was a little drunk. She was on her third beer when the first guest came twenty minutes ago and hadn't stopped yet.

Surprisingly how punctual men can become when sex is promised, she thought. Each one was told that they were going to get some tonight and that others would be there. However, they weren't sure exactly what was going on.

Pete was first to comment on the guests. He said, "Four guys and you're the only chick in this room. What do you have planned Kelly? Are you planning to take us all on?" All four of them looked at her.

"Well my favorite word is 'gangbang'," she said wryly. She was getting wet just thinking about being serviced by all four studs in the room, or maybe it was the way Jim was massaging her feet. Maybe it was a combination of them. For whatever reason she couldn't help but to think about the four hidden dicks in the room. She knew what she just said just gave them a little stir.

"So you like getting it on with more than one guy at a time?" Pete said.

"That's my girl," Joe said, "the little nymph. Never met a penis that she couldn't make hard."

She giggled and smiled. The body language of the guys informed her that they certainly weren't opposed to gang banging her. It was also obvious that she was getting aroused.

Kelly smiled, peered directly into Joe's eyes, and then let her eyes travel down to his crotch. Yep, he was getting hard. She licked her lips.

"So have you been to bed with more than one guy before? At the same time?"

"Hell yes."

There was a round of cheers from the guys.

"What's the most people that you've been naked with at the same time?"

"Two guys and a guy and a girl."

"What's that like?"

"F'ing hot! I was constantly being touched or sucked or fucked. And the other woman had really big breasts, so there were fun to play with."

"You're bi?"

"Of course, isn't everyone to some degree? Everyone has thoughts of doing it with someone of the same sex." She let her words hang then laughed at the tension and nervous expressions on the guy's faces; especially Pete's. "I just acted on them. Several times. Actually, more than a few times." She laughed. "I'm a bit of a slut."

"Ah...no kidding," Joe said, "Sorry, I didn't mean to..."

She cut him off. "Don't apologize. It is true."

She took a swig of beer.

"You're a nymph, not a slut," Pete said. "There is a difference. You're very selective with who you sleep with. You only sleep with the best." The other guys toasted that.

"That's true." She stretched. "Do you know what I want?"

"We have an idea."

"I want to four of you to pick me up, carry me into the bedroom and ravish me. None of the queer faggot stuff, I want to be the centre of attention. There's a box of condoms sitting on the dresser."

Smiles all around, but nobody moved until Kelly said, "Well?"

"Sounds like fun," Pete said.

"Well..."she raised her hand and fired a make-believe gun," Go!"

Without hesitation the four of them approached her and she was airborne. Somebody was feeling her ass and rubbing her crotch while somebody else was cupping her left tit. She had been stripped naked before she was placed on the bed. Somebody was sliding his tongue all the way up her pussy. Her eyes were clenched, but she knew that it had to be Jim. 'He likes doing that," she thought. John was sucking on her nipples and Pete was rubbing his hard penis in her face. Automatically she engulfed it and let her tongue roam. She didn't know where Joe was until she felt another penis rub against her cheek.

Jim entered her and she grabbed Joe's penis.

"Go like mad guy," John said, taking on the roll of team captain. "Cum then let the next guy ride her."

From then on it was a blur of ecstasy. John who was followed by Pete, then finally Jim followed Joe. She wasn't sure who was who, it all felt very good. Each one rode hard and fast until they came. A few of them even took a second turn. Her pussy has never taken such an intensive pounding.

Her favorite moment was when he was riding Pete in the reverse cowgirl position, Jim was playing with her clitoris with his tongue, John was sucking her breasts and Joe was French kissing her. It was total pleasure. Slowly she rocked Pete's penis and reached out and took Joe's and John's penis in her hands. It was a toss up to see who was harder between them and Pete. She wondered if Jim was hard too. Knowing him he probably was, she thought.

She stood under the shower, eyes closed, head back and let all the remains of sex wash off her body while enjoying the soothing caress of the water. She wondered when too much is really too much. Good question, she thought. I've had enough sex for now.

Sometime during her orgy, the phone had rang and someone had left a message. After her shower, she listened to the message and laughed when Daniel said, "It's me. I'm just wondering what you're up to?"

The last person she wanted to talk to was Daniel so she ignored him. Heck, she thought. It was too late to call him anyways.

And besides, she was tired and just wanted to go to bed.

He called her at work and she made small talk for a few minutes then said that she had work to do. He asked her what was wrong and she replied, "Nothing. I'm just busy."

After work he came over unannounced that made her want to break `free' from him even more.

Again, he asked her what was wrong. He pressured her far too much and she snapped. "Last night I screwed four guys at the time," she said bitterly.

"No?"

"If you don't believe me, check the waste basket for the soiled condoms."

"What you had an orgy and you didn't call me?"

"It was a non-bi party."

He glared at her. He was mad. "You have a problem with bisexuals." It was a statement not a question.

"Yes fag." Even she couldn't believe her harsh words.

"I can handle other guy part, but don't ever call me that."

Defiantly she looked him in the eye and said, "Queer boy." With those words, she knew that she had crossed the line.

Without saying a word, he left and the door announced that he was mad as hell. After the walls stopped vibrating from the slamming door there was silence.

For the next few days she heard nothing from him,

not even a phone call. She felt numb with anger at first, and then it was replaced with panic. She was letting go of someone who she really liked, despite a few issues. Also, she knew that he was good for her. Well, not that gay stuff, but all the other things were good. Well, mostly.

She laid awake on the third night without him and stared at the ceiling. A conversation she had with Sara about her lifestyle came to mind. She said, "Women tend to be cautious about who they have sex with because they're the ones who get invaded. They feel that they're the ones opening up a large part of themselves and one vulnerable. I say it is the opposite. It is the guy who is taking the risk. He's the one who sticks his neck out – so to speak – by intrusting me with is dick." She giggled." He might not get it back. He's the one who gives up something."

"You're drunk."

"Yep.

They both laughed.

"But the thing is the whole danger of getting pregnant thing."

"What with the pill?"

"True. Okay then disease."

"Condoms."

"Violence."

"Just avoid creeps. I always find a nice guy who I say to, "I think that you're just a nice guy who wants to get laid. If you treat me like a lady you're in.""

"That seems to work for you. You're pretty good at reading people."

"Well, we see the nasty side of men everyday. After a while those types are easy to spot."

"Unfortunately, not all women are as good as you about spotting them."

"Sadly no," she said seriously then to lighten the mood again added, "that is why I'm the Dead Sperm Collector and they're not."

Sara laughed. "Oh boy. We should get you a badge."

"So I can flash it to cute guys."

"Yes."

"You'll be an instant heroin cause you know how guys are always going on about how they need to release all the built up dead sperm."

"Yes. Dead Sperm Collector here."

"You can waltz into a bar with your Dead Sperm Collector badge and come to their rescue."

Kelly laughed as the image played like a movie in her head. Seriously, she said, "You know what it all comes down to, eh?"

"What?"

"Sex feels so damn good. And men aren't afraid to admit it. That is why they want it all the time."

"That is true."

"And that is why, I like it and I'm not afraid of being promiscuous. I like to have sex! I love sex! I never want to stop. I don't care if the whole world knows it. I'm a slut in their eyes I guess, but I don't care. Call me what they will – they're going to anyways – I'm having fun."

"Hmmm…fair enough. I still would like to see you stick with one – or more – regular partners and no more strangers."

"Dually noted. In fact I've been slowly building a list of regulars."

"Oh god you sound like a pro."

Kelly laughed. "Oh boy."

"Don't you want someone to grow old with?"

"I don't care. I just want to get nailed as often as possible. If I meet someone special great, but I'm more than a little tired of spending a lot of time dating a guy only to find out that they're defective in some ways and I don't mean physically."

"We're all defective. You just have to find someone whose quirks you can live with."

Quirks, Kelly mused.

She called Daniel and since he didn't pick up, she left a message. "I'm sorry for insulting you like I did. That was wrong of me. I don't know why I was so angry. Call me when you can."

She knew exactly why she was so angry. The conflict was eating at her nerves. This fact he had to know regardless of what happened next.

He called back and accepted her apology, but he wasn't warm and friendly as he usually was. She asked him what was wrong. "Well, I'm really pissed off that you had a gang bang without me."

"I can see your point."

"So why did you do it then?"

"Um…"

"Well?"

"Maybe it is best if I told you in person."

He groaned.

"Daniel. I need you to come over please."

"Okay, I'll be right over."

She told him about her conflict and as he listened, he nodded his head. Every once in awhile, he commented, "That makes sense."

"So, do you see why I did it?"

"Yes, I do," he said. "It doesn't make it right, but I can see the problem."

"That's good, I guess."

"Well, it all depends what you want out of life. Make a decision and decide to live with it."

She nodded her head. "So, where does that leave us?"

"Where do you want to leave it?"

"I know that I want you in my life."

He smiled.

"And I'm sorry that I did it. I guess that I was just overreacting to you. I promise never to do it again."

"Well, you can, just <u>invite</u> me next time."

She nodded and smiled. She started to cry.

"Hey, don't do that."

"Why not?" She said between sobs.

"Because you have to tell me about it and I don't want you to be upset by it."

She looked shocked and stunned. "You want to hear about it?"

"Every detail."

"Oh."

She gave him the set up and when she got to the part of her being carried to the bed, he stopped her. "Come here," he said. He undid and lowered his pants. He was hard as a rock. "Suck me as you continue. Consider it part of your punishment."

On her knees in front of him, she continued. "I had a tongue inside of me…" she gave him a few good strokes with her mouth and tongue. "…while I was sucking on a penis…"

"How big was it?"

"Seven inches."

"And the one inside of you?"

"Nine." She went back to sucking.

"Nice. How turned on were you?"

She took a break long enough to say: "Extremely turned on."

"How many orgasms?"

"I lost count after five."

"Do you want to do it again?"

"God yes!" She was now sucking his penis with intense passion. Both of them were turned on by her orgy. She would add a few words here and there between sucks. She said, "And woman too," and "and anything goes."

He came.

A week later, the phone rang and she didn't recognize the number. Hesitantly, she picked up. "Hello?"

It was Gail. After small talk, they agreed to meet for coffee on Thursday. This excited Kelly and she told Daniel who she was and what she had tried to do. "See if she can change his mind. It sounds like fun."

"And new territory for us."

When Gail walked in, Kelly's mouth watered. Seeing Gail's large breasts straining against the blouse brought back some pleasant memories. It also reinforced the fact that Kelly was indeed bisexual. She wanted to jump her right then and there.

"I've missed you," Gail said. "I really enjoyed our little get together."

"Me too."

"Steve finally told me that you phoned. And he told me what it was about. I'm sorry that he said no."

"I wished that I had phoned you instead. Something tells me that you would have said yes."

Gail didn't have to answer that question. "It sounds like fun."

"Sex is fun." Her eyes were in full bedroom mode now. "It is adult playtime."

Gail looked around to see if anyone was within earshot. "Let's take a walk."

They walked along the strip mall until there wasn't anyone else around. "Steve doesn't want me to be with another guy, but he doesn't mind if I get it on with another woman."

"I know, some men are funny that way."

"Um…"

"Shhh." Kelly put a finger to Gail's lips and licked her own. "I know. I want you too."

"But we have a problem. You can only sleep with someone if your boyfriend is around and I'm not allowed to sleep with another guy."

"That is a problem. Come." She led her around the corner where she planted a huge kiss on her. Gail was right into it and didn't hold back. Her hands pawed Kelly's thighs and hips. Kelly moaned as she gripped Gail's oversized breasts. "So nice," she said.

Gail broke it off, pulled up her shirt and pulled Kelly's head into her breasts. The bra had a front latch, which Kelly undid. She sucked on them with unabashed passion. Her hand found it's way into Gail's pants then into her panties. She slid her finger into her pussy and let it absorb the moister from the surroundings. Once wet, she glided her finger upwards to her clitoris. She flickered it slowly at first then slowly increased the speed until she came.

"Thank you," Gail said as she was reassembling

her clothes. "That was very good. I will do you now."

Kelly shook her head. "No, I should go."

"You okay?"

"I shouldn't have done that."

"I know. Sorry." She flashed her cute little smile. Kelly melted. She wanted to be free to ravish this woman all night.

Guilt! Even though she didn't really do much, she felt terrible.

That evening she couldn't sleep. Despite the long talk with Daniel, she felt trapped and bored and had itchy feet. She contemplated getting up and marching into the Pussy Pub to get hammered and nailed by some stranger. Have sex with a total stranger! That still appealed to her, but she knew that Matt would see her and tell Daniel. And besides she would know that she had done it. Guilt.

"Ugh!" She groaned at her internal conflict.

She started to touch herself. At least, she thought. Daniel didn't put any restrictions on her being with herself.

She stopped. She knew that she was angry. At that

point she knew that she

couldn't do it. She was who she was and that was that. She couldn't be faithful to anyone not even to a sex machine like Daniel.

"Fuck it," she said.

She got dressed and was in the Pub just before closing time.

"Hi Kel," Matt said.

She sat at the bar and studied the scenery. Matt noticed her wandering eye and came over. He smiled at her. "I get off in a while," he said.

She smiled and licked her lips. Her eyes wandered to his body. She longed to rub her hands on his six-pack and to her it felt like an eternity until he was walking her home.

He waited until they got to her place before he dropped the bomb. "Listen, Daniel is crazy about you and I can't let you blow it," he said.

"What?"

"Go to bed. Alone."

She got angry. "You fag! You purposely led me on so I couldn't score tonight."

"Yes, I did."

"I hate you! Get out!"

He left and she went to bed not feeling great about herself. It took until the next day to realize the favor that Matt had done. She wanted to apologize to him and decided that it was best done in person so she went to the bar after dinner. When she walked in she spotted Daniel sitting at the bar. She almost left, but he saw her. She didn't know how to explain to Daniel what she wanted to say to Matt, so she pretended that everything was okay, had a drink with Daniel and waited for him to go to the washroom.

"Matt," she said. "Thank you for that talk last night. I owe you."

"No problem."

When he came back, Daniel asked, "Kelly. Can we talk?"

"About what?"

"Well…us."

She didn't want to because she was frustrated and tormented by the conflict within her. This pressured something inside that was already at the boiling point so she decided once and for all to blow this guy off, the source the conflict. No Daniel. No conflict. And she knew exactly how to do it. The truth. She was a mega-slut. "Listen guy, what would you say if I said that I've slept with just about every guy in this place, hmmm?"

"Have you?"

"Yes," she said definitely, expecting him to freak out. He nodded his head then motioned to the guy at the pool table.

He nodded his head. "How about him?"

"Yes."

"When?"

"About four months ago, we were both in here late. Nice guy." She squinted her eyes and with an added dose of defiance said, "Big dick. Good times."

Again, he nodded and while calmly looking into her eyes asked, "Did you cum? Did you get off?"

"Yes," she said, with a stunned expression on her face, but with defiance still in her voice.

"How about the good looking guy in the corner."

"Three weeks ago," she said normally.

"Was it better than the first guy?"

"Ah…" Her mouth was agape.

"Who is the best in here?"

She looked puzzled. She knew that it was Daniel. "You really want to know, why?"

He shrugged his shoulders. "Why not?"

She peered at him. "You're strange."

"What? Why would you say that?"

"Because I think that not only don't you mind that I've fucked most of the bar, but I think that it turns you on. You have a boner right now don't you?"

He smiled. "Guilty."

"Really." She slid off her shoe, slid down in the chair so that her foot could reach his crotch. Her toes felt stiffness. "Wow!"

He moved as she continued to softly tease her erection.

"Well, let me tell who the second best fuck is in here."

"Yes, please."

"See that body builder who just walked in."

"Yes."

"Well, he has an enormous penis. Twelve inches at least. The guy isn't good in bed at all but I didn't care. I did all the work. Once I got him home on my couch I deep throated him, while my right hand jerked at the base of his shaft and my left worked in between them. And you know what? In total I think that I only covered half of it. It is a monster."

"Wow, that's big." He looked over at the body builder and studied his body. "So you prefer massive dicks?"

"Normally no, but it was the thrill of the moment." She increased her foot rubbing and he approved. "God, it was a thick long perfectly structured shaft."

"Go on."

"I slurped on that thing like it was a Popsicle on a hot summer's day. My salvia ran down it to my left hand and helped lube that section then down to the base. God, it was beautiful, so thick and strong.

He jerked and suppressed a moan as she touched his hard penis.

"Wow, I wonder who the best is cause I'm not sure I can take it."

She pointed and smiled at him. He reached over and put his hand on hers. "Listen Kelly," he said. "I'm nuts about you. I want to be with you. What can I do or don't do or change that would please you?"

"Well," she said. "Do you really want to know?"

"I think that I need to know. Good or bad. I just need to know why I'm pushing you away."

"For one stop being so pushy about things. I want to make some of the decisions."

"Okay, I can do that. Done."

"Don't be so intense. Calm down a little. There is a word called, patience."

"I have heard that there is," he said wryly.

"Yes."

"Okay, will work on that."

"Really?"

"I will try and I will succeed with your help."

This brought a smile to her face.

He leaned over to hug her. She surrendered into his arms. To her this felt as good as any fuck that she has had. She needed tenderness right now. She rested her head on his chest. "I have another confession to make," she said.

"It is okay, tell me it all."

She told him everything that had happened with Gail and how guilty she felt. As if that wasn't enough, she added the bit about her wanting to get hammered and nailed by some stranger and what Matt had done for her, for them. She broke down and started to cry.

"I'm so sorry," she said between sobs.

"The part with Gail I can forgive you for," he said. "Actually, it sounds really

hot. Maybe we can work it out where I can watch you two from a distance. Maybe go parking with her and…"

"Or how about you hide in the closet or something?"

"That would work."

She smiled and dried her eyes. "You don't mind?"

"Okay, that problem is solved. The part that concerns me is that you were tempted to pick up your old habits. That wouldn't be good."

"No, it wouldn't." She started crying again.

"What is it that appeals to you, the thrill of the unknown? The danger? What?"

"I guess that I'm just promiscuous." She looked sad. "I just get really hot and bothered when I'm trying to determine if the guy has a big or small one. I guess that it is the thrill of the undiscovered country. And guys are so grateful for a quickie."

"That's true. I know that I am."

"The problem with being in a relationship – no matter how wonderful the other person is and your are Daniel– is that things – especially the sex part – falls into a routine, and routine means boredom."

"Sounds like you've had one too many boring relationships – the sex part at least."

"Or if the sex part isn't boring then it's just a sexual relationship. It's one or the other. No balance."

"That has been my problem as well, but with you I think that I have reached that balance."

She lifted her head from his chess to say: "Daniel. I will make love to you anytime, anyplace and I never want that to stop, but I can't help who I am. I know I can't have it both ways."

Daniel thought for a minute then said, "Why not?"

"Why not what?

"Have it both ways. Heck, I like guys too and I can relate to the thrill that you experience by picking up strangers. God knows I've done it myself. So why don't we try it. The next time that you get the urge, let's go out and pick up an unknown penis and suck it together." He laughed.

"Really?" She stopped crying.

"Sure, why not? It sounds like fun. It will take more work because some guys just won't like me being along. Or maybe I can come home and surprise you two then join in. That would work too. Planned of course. Hmmm. Ideas are coming."

She cupped her hand on his cheek and softly planted a kiss on his lips. "You're wonderful."

"No, I'm bi and oversexed, just like you. So I understand."

She rested her head against his chest. "And I've found my soul mate. You made me realize how lonely I was before I met you."

He rolled his eyes. She was getting mushy, which was totally unlike her. He didn't mind though. "Ah, Kelly."

"Yeah."

He pointed to a guy just walking in. "How about him?"

Kelly studied the man sitting at the table near the pool table. He was squarely built, short dark hair, strong chin and with blue eyes.

"He is cute," she said.

"I think so too."

"Really?

"Yes." He leaned over and whispered in her ear: "Go screw him."

She couldn't believe that not only could she actually sleep with the nice piece of meat that she was staring at, but had permission to do, providing that Daniel was there too.

She looked into Daniel's green eyes. For a moment he was looking elsewhere. Her mind wondered. God, she thought. I can do anything that I want and this guy won't get upset. In fact, he will get turned on by it. He is a freak. And…my god, I'm a freak as well. I have been promiscuous and alone and I have had someone and been bored. Now I can remain promiscuous and have someone, the best of both worlds.

Her body told her that she liked the idea of all this. She was getting turned on and her mind started to wonder. She was making out with that the cute guy in the back of a car. Daniel was driving and watching in the rear view mirror as best that he could. The guy's hands were roaming and she was moaning. One hand had manoeuvred under her

blouse, undid her bra and was playing with her breasts while the other hand went downtown. It had squeezed its way in between her legs and was now rubbing her crotch through her jeans. This caused her to kiss him harder. Her tongue probed his mouth and battled with his tongue.

She broke off the kiss and said, "Fuck me."

"We're almost home," Daniel said.

"I can't wait." She lifted her ass to pull off her jeans. The guy gladly helped.

Daniel pulled into a parking lot of a closed laundry. He drove around the back where it was dark, but not too dark. He wanted to see the action.

And Kelly didn't disappoint. After her pants were off she got to work on his. First she rubbed the bulge with her hand then with her face, rubbing like a cat rubs against her owner's leg when it wants something. This drove him crazy. He undid her pants and pulled them down. To drive him further over the edge, she tried to deep throat the bulge in the underwear.

"Here buddy," Daniel said as he held out a condom.

The guy took it as Kelly leaned back in the seat and spread her legs. Half crazed with anticipation he

stumbled putting it on.

While waiting, Daniel wetted his thumb leaned over and played with Kelly's pussy. She smiled at him. "Hurry up buddy," Daniel said, "Kelly wetter than the ocean."

"Got it."

He manoeuvred between her legs and slid it in. He rode with intensity as Kelly hung on. Periodically she would look up to see Daniel's gleaming face. She didn't see him do it, but she knew that he was playing with himself in the front seat.

"When he's done," Daniel said. "I'm next."

She smiled.

Her next vision was lying in bed with Daniel teaching that oversized actor guy how to please a women. Daniel would explain a technique, do it for a while then actor boy would try it. Then...

She snapped back to reality. "I can't believe that you would let me screw him," she said.

"Anything you want that make you happy," he said. "Let's just have fun. Whoever we pick up, we pick up <u>together</u> and enjoy <u>together</u>."

She smiled because she knew that this might work. "Promiscuous together!"

ABOUT THE AUTHOR

Rachel Richards is an oversexed redhead who loves adult playtime and spends her time writing and doing "research" for her erotic novels. Her novels Kindle are:

`*Swinger Sex Games'*: a couple invents ways of seducing other couples.

`*Kelly's Wild Side'*: Prelude to `*Into the Swing'*. This is the story of how Kelly and Daniel got together.

`*Into the Swing'*: after a number of false starts, Kelly and Daniel enter into the swinging lifestyle.

`*Full Swing'*: Kelly and Daniel go deeper into the lifestyle and attend their first orgy.

`*50 Shades of Gay'*: an older woman seduces a beautiful young woman into the lesbian world.

`*More 50 Shades of Gay'*: a young beautiful woman experiments with both men and women to determine which sex she prefers.

`*The Promiscuous Games'*: a parody of the Hunger Games where people compete to see who can out sex the other. Only the winner can continue having sex.

`*Confessions of a Gym Teacher'*: Beth Porter is a

gym teacher who is tricked into sleeping with some of her older students. Note: all characters are over 18 years of age.

All titles are available as eBooks by Blue Ops on Kindle. The following are Blue Ops Titles by Rachel that are available on all eBook formats:

Into the Swing

Swinger Sex Games

Slut Wife

The following are titles by Blue Ops author Dick Talent:

Swinging Vacation

I Married a Nympho

Some of the above titles will be coming to paperback soon.

www.ingramcontent.com/pod-product-compliance
Lightning Source LLC
Chambersburg PA
CBHW051535260626
47170CB00003B/947